Ramblings of an Old Teenager

A novel

By
Rumbi Chen

*To Catherine Dunduru, the protagonist of her own novel,
and to Reuben Dunduru, whose spirit lives on.*

Acknowledgments

It is not my intention to leave out anyone, but if I have done so, apologies.

I wish to extend my deepest gratitude to the memory of my late grandfather, Sekuru Maponga son of Swarabhoy, whose rich tales and traditional wisdom have been the cornerstone of this book. His legacy of storytelling lives on in these pages.

To my beloved grandmother Gogo Maponga "*Wekuzvigunwe*", whose faith and prayers have been a constant source of strength, I am profoundly thankful. Your unwavering belief in me, coupled with the wisdom you imparted, have been invaluable.

To my parents, siblings, and extended family, both near and far, your prayers, support, and encouragement, steeped in both tradition and faith, have sustained me throughout this journey.

To Trudy for the infinite explanations, Ony, Nel ten Wolde and Reinout Quispel for the mathematical functions, Munya, Kule Tangai, Mhamha Dorothy, Chenge, Max, Gamu, Diana *muzukuru* weVaShawasha, Kumbi, Baba Da, Dorry, Baba Kuku, Baba Nyasha, Mr Phiri, Ty, Tambu and Tatenda, I am blessed to have you all by my side.

To my mum, who patiently answered my myriad of questions, whether directly or through Mhamha Wenna or my sisters, your unwavering support and guidance have been invaluable throughout this journey. Thank you for your endless patience and wisdom.

To my late dad, your enduring wisdom and love remain ever-present in my heart. Though you are no longer with us, your guidance has profoundly shaped me. I am forever grateful for the stories, lessons you taught and the love you shared.

I am indebted to Mhamha Wenna for her love, guidance, and patience in explaining complex matters I asked. Your prayers and support mean more to me than words can express.

To Mr. Muusha, my perpetual mentor, a remarkable author by virtue, thank you for your Christian counsel and insightful guidance, which have shaped both my development and my writing. Your influence has been immeasurable.

I am appreciative of Dr Simbarashe Victor Masarirambi's Christian leadership and spiritual guidance. He graciously offered clarity on matters such as the will of God and tradition, enlightening my path with wisdom and understanding. For all the teachings which helped me in several aspects from Mai Sauti, Pastor Banda, Apostle Keith, Prophet Madiro and Evangelist Malvern, I am grateful.

To my fellow writer @Pope (Francis Muzofa) whose light-hearted banter brought joy and laughter to the writing process, thank you for your literary friendship and support.

Lastly, to my beta readers, whose traditional or Christian faith, along with their constructive feedback, have helped refine this manuscript, I am immensely grateful. Your input has been instrumental in shaping this book into its final form.

To Mr. Tendai Sauta, for his encouragement, editing work, and insightful reviews, I extend my heartfelt thanks.

To everyone who has contributed, whether through tradition or faith, your presence and influence have been instrumental in bringing this book to fruition. May God bless you abundantly.

Thank you,
Rumbi

"...I believe, therefore, I speak..."

Chapter 1

Not all answers are solutions
Mother's mother, Eti

Mbuya Zvirevo's reedy voice woke her up. Mbuya Zvirevo? That was not a good sign. Danger! Mbuya Zvirevo started shaking and growling in an uncontrollable manner and in an instant, she began to chant endless incantations.

Zivai mumbled, "This bad omen has everything to do with my baby, after losing a husband, what could be worse?"

Finally, something came out of Mbuya Zvirevo's endless gibberish, she murmured, "Sometimes the life we bring is the same life that will take us out of this world. We can never be sure of what our children will become until we see what they become. These flowers we raise will rise against us beyond levels we ever rose to. The sad thing is that we cannot tell at birth, only in death do we realise what these flowers really were. This child will cause great misery."

With one last roar, Mbuya Zvirevo shook violently and bowed down in silence. Nobody dared probe her, that was for another day. Her giant stature enhanced her appeal as the chosen one by the ancestors. She commanded respect across the whole plain. However, not everyone agreed with her life-style and her utterances. Tradition had to prevail; she was merely a conduit. She did not choose this, she was chosen.

The old village spirit medium had spoken. Her words never failed, or rather, had never failed.

At once, Zivai sighed, whistled and writhed. Was it not enough that she had lost her husband? Now, her son too? Moreover, in a few days her infamous brother-in-law would marry her. No sane woman would be excited about marriage under these circumstances. Worse still, being inherited by that unwashed, uncouth yet handsome wanderer. Her nightmare was just becoming longer. Zivai knew like everyone else that tradition had to prevail. She simply had to watch and be an excited spectator cheering as her life crept by, with her fate being dribbled by others.

In a flash, an ailing frail woman grabbed Zivai's baby and disappeared into the thick morning fog. Zivai, in her weak state, managed to raise her left arm in a bid to at least lay hold of the woman's garment. She fainted in shock. By the time an alarm was raised, the whole village was awash with folk running indiscriminately. The villagers were astounded; several theories arose explaining the motive behind such an act.

"It was that witch Marujata!" one eyewitness shouted. Murmurs in the crowd were in support of this assertion. After all, Marujata was a self-proclaimed witch who had enemies even beyond the village. Just that no individual had caught her red-handed to warrant accusation charges. How she was present in Zivai's hut was a mystery. She was known for devouring foetuses before their births. Expecting women avoided her at all costs. They would not even allow her to cast sight of their bulging tummies. Apparently, she inherited sorcery from her grandmother who raised her after being orphaned. Several individuals argued it was a divine encounter, someone trying to prevent the bad omen heralded by Mbuya Zvirevo. In their small groups, they whispered that the only way was to kill the infant. Nobody dared show their inward happiness at this possibility, they already feared for their future and any relief was welcome. Whichever way it came.

"Why not inquire of Mbuya and stop this?" some searchers mumbled. Well, the spirit medium only spoke when she had a message. Hurried footsteps were all over the place. There were little feet scurrying in the bushes rummaging the undergrowth. Overhead, angry voices filled the thick air. Amongst the confusion, a whirlwind approached with so much gait it picked a rabbit and a chick along its trajectory. The locals viewed whirlwinds as harbingers of misfortune. Small voices chuckled in the distance as most of the people's faces had white eyebrows from the resulting dust.

"There she is!" Uncle Zano shouted, and a mob followed the direction of his twisted finger. He led the chase being the one with long strides. Surprisingly, a plump man manoeuvred in the undergrowth and flew onto Marujata. Clutching Zivai's baby by the waist, Marujata's face crushed against the thorns, and she let go of the bundled-up infant while she writhed in pain. A leggy man leaped with outstretched arms ensuring the baby landed safely. What a dramatic welcome onto mother earth. Meanwhile, the furious throng pounced on the perpetrator and a stampede followed. The crowd was uncontrollable and nobody could silence them. A loud cheer engulfed the air, there was loud cheering and jeering as others chanted "witch, witch, thief!" How any sane person could commit such a heinous act was baffling.

It was taboo for men to manhandle or touch women unless necessary or by way of an emergency rescue. However, in this instance, two men grabbed Marujata's arms and walked her to the chief's homestead. Meanwhile, Mangondi whispered to his cronies a rumour that Mbuya Zvirevo had staged her trance, so she emerges a hero in the charade. The word spread like the crushing white waters of the Mara. In a bid to gain favour with Mangondi, as most of the village ladies were attracted to him, Emma had to outshine the rest. She blasted, "Utter nonsense. This is a ridiculous coincidence that you proclaim something sinister, and it happens in seconds. Well planned Mbuya Zvirevo or rather, Eti. You have outdone yourself this time, stooping so low." Emma looked around nodding her had scanning for approval. Acting in one voice, the elderly women with crooked backs seized Mbuya Zvirevo. It was amazing they had immense power to grab her or maybe she had allowed them to. Nevertheless, most of the crowd criticised these allegations as baseless and stemming from jealousy and fear of being exposed. However, a few staunch Mangondi admirers mumbled and pushed her around pointing accusing fingers at her. Pointing fingers at someone was considered the highset display of disrespect. They booed at her for conniving with Marujata and threatened to send her before the chief, who happened to be her uncle. Mangondi sensitised women around him saying that it was part of Mbuya Zvirevo's grand plan to create a problem and then purport to bring a solution all in a bid to win people's hearts.

"She wins because of favouritism and nepotism. We must deal with her ourselves, taking her there will not help us. It strengthens her, remember last rainy season when the cattle ate the chief's maize field. He did not reprimand her or demand compensation," reasoned Mangondi, the brains of his group.

"Maybe the king's court will yield victory for us, he loves money that one," a bald man suggested this while rubbing his moustache. He took pride in his long grey moustache such that each time he drank opaque beer, he laughed at the layer of residue on his moustache. He liked how the hair floated and swam in the beer. Others said he used his moustache to spike people's drinks. The moment he saw his moustache in the cup he would not drink again and that raised suspicion. He was Mangondi's closest disciple.

"Your indignation still baffles me. Let us go to the chief right now," Mbuya Zvirevo said her voice stern and composed. She knew too well her brother's aim and as long as she lived, he would not prevail. In fact, even in her death, she claimed he would not win, for evil would cower before good.

Emma clutched Mbuya Zvirevo's firm hand which was greenish from crushing various medicinal herbs for Zivai. Emma hissed insults at her as she led the delegation to the chief's courtyard.

A growing noise alerted the chief as the crowd drew closer to his homestead. Every week there was chaos in the village and Mangondi featured in almost all the cases, it began to irritate the chief. He squinted his eyes to narrow his gaze and sighed when he noticed his niece Mbuya Zvirevo. His mouth curled up as his mind raced to the last message she gave him, concerning his chieftaincy which had eventually happened, all in a peaceful manner. His smile withered the moment he spotted Mangondi whose physique was both attractive and grotesque. Ladies only loved him for his engrossing drumming and his broad veined gigantic palms with tufts of hair on the three inner knuckles. He sulked before feigning a smile.

"Gentlemen, welcome. Good morning respected ladies," he said clapping to which everyone clapped back. It was unusual for the esteemed chief to greet visitors first, instead, the norm was the opposite. He did this when he wanted his courtyard vacated in no time and only clever calculating people figured this pattern. He dismissed their case on the grounds of time of day and circumstances. It was taboo to accuse a medium of such a heinous act when they were the custodians of humanity. Mbuya Zvirevo muffled a laugh. She winked at Emma and Mangondi at the same time one eye for each of them. Mangondi shivered and snarled. He punched the ground sending a thin layer of dust into the air, before spitting and scooping the sputum and dust paste and licking it. His bald crony sniggered as he patted him on the right shoulder. Mangondi grinned, "You know what to do."

* * *

At midday Mbuya Zvirevo picked twigs piled further outside her kitchen to prepare *mashakada* to comfort Zivai. *Mashakada* was a delicacy in these parts of the country. It was a rice dish mashed with heaps of peanut butter. However, Mbuya Zvirevo's love of peanut butter cascaded down to her grandchildren. It was no surprise this meal was also their comfort food. Mbuya Zvirevo now stocked her firewood a stone throw from her kitchen which was rather an inconvenience. After last summer's incident in which her visiting aunt carried a vine snake camouflaged on twigs, she never placed them straight into her hut. Instead, she let the sun, and the elements treat them so any intruders would slither or fly away, only then would she pick them in small batches into the hut. It is only the thick firewood she stored away in the barn and out in the open. She was not afraid of snakes nor anything known or unknown to man, but for her visitors' sake and safety, she had to take such precautions. However, unknown to her, the bald man, under instruction, had been near her kitchen where the dishes hung to dry. He knew what to do. Crashed glass on moustache. Ground glass so smooth you could not see it unless you had bulging eyes like Mangondi's.

* * *

Mbuya Zvirevo busied herself cooking *mashakada* using the finest unrefined rice and smooth peanut butter, which Tarisai ground for her the previous day. Mbuya Zvirevo took pride in showing off her farming skills. Each time she harvested rice, she would pound about half of it whilst storing the rest for the coming dry season. She spoilt her visitors with a cup of the maroon coloured rice which mashed well when cooked. "*Du du muduri* (, *katswe,* Eti *muduri, katswe, katswe.* Tarisai *muduri, katswe…* (*du, du,* in the mortar, *katswe,* Eti get into the mortar, *katswe, katswe, katswe.* Tarisai, in the mortar, *katswe…*" The "du, du" described the sound of the pestle hitting against the mortar and *katswe* was the responsorial word. Tarisai would sing as she often volunteered grinding or pestling. She got to enjoy the song and in her early years, she would look into the mortar thinking the song is instructing her to look inside. She was too young to comprehend that her name was both a verb and a noun. At one time she toppled into the mortar, so much for being off-balance and short. Well, now she was still short and stout with charming three dimples all on one side. Her peers made fun of her, and she cried, until one day when she stood up for herself.

Meanwhile, the warm aroma of peanut butter flew in my direction and spiralled with intent into my nostrils, I could not ignore the call. I followed my feet to the three-legged pot which had enough to feed the entire village excluding children.

I had just arrived at my mother's homestead to comfort her on the earlier nuisances. Zivai and my mother had an amicable relationship typical of first granddaughter and granny. I knew without a doubt my mother would never intentionally harm me, let alone my children. To even imagine that she could connive with anyone to harm us was appalling. Those village rogues were so jealous that they would do anything to tarnish her image. It was the work of pure jealousy, hatred and cruelty. Quite diabolical to think of it. These haters' efforts were gaining popularity and that was starting to disturb me. Nevertheless, trying to comfort my mother was a mere formality, knowing how stoic she could be. Mother was sophisticated, stoic, stubborn and sassy despite being modest.

"Nothing beats my peanut butter, whether smooth or crunchy. Very soon David Livingstone's statue will be here," Mbuya Zvirevo bragged with a careless laugh while her eyes sparkled making her look half her age. That radiance flushed her cheeks for a while before she retorted, "Did you see those monkeys? It is unbelievable."

I sneered, "We are all monkeys but, those were hungry ones. There is not even a morsel of food in their kitchens which is why they disturbed the sleeping sun with their unfounded rubbish."

We both cried with laughter and mother added, "Speaking of which, your little monkey is now a peanut butter expert. She is the one—"

A sharp scream accompanied by a continuous trail of weeping stupefied Mbuya Zvirevo. On impulse, we sped towards the source of the deafening cry. The short distance to the backyard between the mulberry trees and the washing area seemed like a journey to Geneva.

Despite being older and weightier, Mbuya Zvirevo arrived ahead of me, which reminded me to resume stretches and jumping jacks at dawn. Unlike mother, I burst into tears when I saw the amount of blood staining the ground and leaves. Mother lifted Tarisai who had fainted and lay her in recovery position and I remembered this from my first aid training at the village centre. Looking at her lifeless body, I wept. These cries alerted villagers who were going about their daily chores in the vicinity. A handful of women and two men rushed into the yard. Instead of helping first, three of the women exchanged questioning eyes. I was too helpless and dejected to confront the gossip mongers. Any other day, it would have turned out nasty after giving them a word or two punches. Although both my mother and I were confrontational, she did not condone violence. I did not care, people had to be taught lessons. My motto was cash talk plus action pack.

"Is she dead?" one nosy woman said pointing at the blood-stained mulberry leaves.

"Shut up, hold yourself," some men reprimanded her. Times of strife and distress call for great calm otherwise a situation can easily spiral out of control."

These men spoke with composure and authority it silenced the nosy woman and the whole crowd. She drooped her head avoiding their gaze, but they shook their heads. The oldest man asked, "Why the exaggeration? We can all see that's not blood, only that trickle there," and he shuffled to help Mbuya Zvirevo nurse the bleeding index finger.

"She is always careful when grinding and pounding. I do not know how this could have happened. I was busy cooking *mashakada* for Zivai who is famished by now. Then I heard the scream." Again, the prying women stared at each other with raised eyebrows and pulled lips. The plump one spat in disdain.

"Will my nail grow back?" Tarisai asked in-between sobs motioning to the tip of her finger which lay in a puddle of blood, mud and debris. Any hungry toddler would have picked it thinking it was a toffee. One stout man picked the little piece and stretched out his hand with conceited effort to mother. I ravished his hand whilst grabbing the finger from his hold.

"Short man, short brains. Now you want to give her that piece, so she completes her rituals!" I yelled staring at him.

The short man clutched his temples and the women exchanged meaningful glares. The norm was outsiders do not intervene in family drama unless it was life threatening. Mother shook her head starting from left, at a tortoise' pace and she washed her hands in mid-air. The last time she shook her head that slow was ten years back and someone died. Tarisai, whose pain had numbed from the leaves mother applied, shouted, "Mum, what's got into you?" I hurt myself doing what I love, leave my granny out of this—"

"Shoosh, you know nothing. You were born yesterday. Let's go," I said clutching her wrist.

"I know lots because He who is in me is greater than you," she shouted back.

She pulled herself away and rushed to grab mother's skirt and hid behind her, peeping. It is said when someone seeks refuge from her elders, that is an automatic truce and anything further is a direct attack on the elder and a curse by default. It is also believed that the resulting curse can be broken by a payment of some sort, be it cattle or cash. I stormed out of the yard, flinging my arms around.

Chapter 2

Mother had remarkable stamina. She maintained composure even at her worst. She did not pass her squabbles onto the next person she met. To her, bygones were indeed gone by. Mother knew me well enough to be bothered by my actions, or perhaps, I had gone a little extreme. I knew that she would never hurt me or my daughters on purpose. But double misfortune in one day, with her at the centre of both events weighed down on my psyche.

I could not stop worrying about Tarisai although I knew she was in safe hands. I feared she would connect her freak accident to that of the leopard and dealing with that was hectic. Once fixated on something, she held onto it until she accomplished her desires.

"Why the sullen look? Zivai's baby is fine," my husband's voice startled me.

"How long have you been standing there for?" I said forcing a smile.

"A caring husband always knows when his wife needs him. I have been at the door long enough to see you bite your nails and to see you chew on your lips."

No doubt he had seen me. I had been too preoccupied to notice his silhouette at the door.

"I am now convinced lightning can strike twice in the same place. I quarrelled with mother again."

"You fought her, not with her."

He was right, mother upheld peace whenever possible, especially with me. Not to say she let people step on her toes. She was quite intentional and assertive, stern yet soft.

I narrated the incident in detail emphasising how the lousy women insinuated that mother had sinister intentions and how that fuelled my baseless anger towards her. By the time I finished explaining, I had already purposed to go and apologise. Despite the general sentiment amongst the villagers that my husband was a coward, there was a calming effect about him. His deep gaze assured me of his full support. He held my mother in such high esteem, he could lay his life for her. Another simple way to maintain harmony in our house was to keep peace with my mother. Either way, I was going to say sorry. I felt happy knowing my decision to go was not out of coercion. My husband and I smiled at each other and that was a perfect signal to show unity of mind.

"Zivai must be awake and famished by now. You go to mother's, and I will go to her," my husband beckoned.

"Mother prepared *mashakada* for her. I will send someone over."

"Oh, she made the country's favourite," my husband chuckled and we laughed at how mother took pride in her unique preparation of this peanut butter specialty.

* * *

Zivai drank tea first to awake her stomach and make way for the heavy meal of *mashakada*. A steaming plate lay next to her and watered her mouth with each breath. In her dire state of hunger, she grabbed the plate and as soon as the food touched her teeth, she spat. My husband shrivelled and before he asked anything, Zivai spluttered.

"You forgot I do not eat rice with a fork. Even blind-folded, I can sniff a fork a metre away." For some strange reason, I never managed to convince Zivai to eat rice with a fork, neither did I understand her rationale for not using one. From the time Zivai became eligible to make her own in-formed food choices, she ditched the fork when eating rice. She argued that using it left her unsatiated. Her weird cardi-nal rule only applied to rice.

* * *

Mother welcomed me in her hut with a nod and sly smile while sniffing some snuff. As if under an invisible push, mother rushed to her feet, took her snuff and scurried out-side. This puzzled me as we were in the middle of my heartfelt apology yet all she said was a paltry, "It is okay, you have done well."

Being the energetic person that I was, I caught up with her within her yard. The snuff was a hint in itself that I should not fret or bombard her with questions. The spirit upon her could be at work, sometimes I could not tell. Each day she became more complex than the previous one.

Meanwhile, the little girl sent with Zivai's food had for-gotten the one instruction she had, to place a spoon in the plate. She put a fork instead. While my husband looked for a spoon, mother banged into Zivai's hut in time to see the little girl handing Zivai a tablespoon.

"Don't eat, Zivai. Wait," Mother shouted. Amidst that momentary confusion, she summoned the small girl to pick two fresh mulberry leaves from outside.

"That is a plate of your demise. He who sent Marujata earlier in the morning is bent on finishing you. This is not your battle. You are a mere accessory of the fact. I am the target here. Even in infancy I was a target," she murmured. Silence ensued as everyone else gasped except the little girl who by virtue of age, failed to comprehend mother's words.

She continued but this time she yelled, "Since when does the end justify the means?"

"Is this your end granny?" the kid broke the silence and handed the leaves to mother who thanked her with a pat on the arm.

Zivai asked, "This is not a riddle, yet I still do not understand." Mother shook her head thrice starting from the right side. That instant, I knew all was well. Calamity averted. On instinct, I ululated, as I had grown accustomed to ever since mother transitioned into Mbuya Zvirevo. From that time, *Ululating* was my second name. I was not her aide though. My second brother's sixth daughter was her assistant but she had visited her cousins beyond the Mudzimundiringe Mountains. Mother beat the butt of her snuffbox on the floor and spilt a few heaps as she chanted some inaudible lyrics. I ululated again, louder. She sandwiched one spoonful of the peanut butter rice on the mulberry leaves which she then held by their stems in opposite directions and rubbed them. By then, everyone's keen gaze lay on her. The leaves had begun to bruise and soon perforations formed.

"If I continue rubbing, they will tatter, you see why. Rice is smooth, but this?"

Awestruck faces followed her every movement as they gasped in horror.

"What material is that? Imagine that in your stomach," my husband said.

Mother answered, "Bring me a dark bowl of hot water. I want this wickedness to speak for itself." She immersed those leaves in a bowl and stirred the water until both leaves were clean and she discarded them. The utter shock on people's faces made them speechless yet curious. Tiny glass particles settled at the bottom. The sparkling glass residue was visible beyond doubt against the dark background of the bowl. I quickly recognised few greenish bits which may have been from Zambezi Lager or Bohlingers Lager beer bottles. Zivai broke into frantic cries speaking in between sobs that she had almost died.

Chapter 3

In her youth, Mbuya Zvirevo was that graceful maiden the whole village admired. Her four brothers bragged about her beauty at every instance they could. She was the epitome of elegance. Her tiny eyes with a slight squint could deceive anyone into thinking she was quiet and shy. Nobody could avoid noticing her giant stature; she literally hovered above her peers.

Mbuya Zvirevo was a nickname she later earned by virtue of her appointment by the ancestral spirits. Her birth name was Eti. A unique one, first of its kind amongst all the clans. Legend has it that my grandfather, Murambiwa, dreamt of being instructed by his father, Chidemo, to name her Eti.

A name fit for a heroine, who in the figure of a lamb would do the feats of a lion. Such a name puzzled even the whiteheads of the village, what they were certain of was that she was destined for greatness, only time would tell. However, Mangondi the first born vowed to never let that greatness flourish. She was meant to be an ordinary house-wife and that was his vow. As a first child, male at that, all manner of greatness had to be bestowed on him alone. Mangondi for all and all for Mangondi.

"Away with Eti," he hissed to himself with clenched fists whenever she was praised for her future prowess. With a hideous face, it wasn't surprising that he had such harsh intentions towards his only sister.

Physically, I didn't resemble my mother except for the husky voice, whereas Tarisai, my second daughter, was a duplicate younger version of her. The curviness, squint eyes, rabbit ears and a sway in their stride, were all similar. Unlike mother, Tarisai was free-spirited, not submissive and her faith off tangent to that of mother. Zivai, my eldest child, was a lanky reserved girl of few words.

Eti was not as simple as most of the local girls of that time were. Also, her marriage was not arranged as she had for some time, been in courtship with the sinewy yet odd-faced Sansirai. Daily they would promenade to the waterhole slightly before daybreak.

They always affirmed in unison, "The rising sun has to revive our love."

At noon, they would relax under the refreshing shade of the *msasa* (Brachystegia spiciformis) trees at the foothill. At dusk, they locked hands, intertwining their fingers to bind their love together with the sleeping sun. The lovebirds believed that as long as the sun rose, their love would remain.

The way Eti's eyes lit whenever Sansirai showered praises, even the sun bore witness. It was unanimously agreed theirs was the ultimate example of a perfect relationship. Even in nearby schools, teachers epitomised them. However, good exists in juxtaposition to bad. A small group of resentful girls ganged up against the village's favourite couple. They couldn't be open about it, they had to be tactful.

"If you think you are now an adult, pack your bag and go this instant!" Emma's mother fumed.

"But mother —"

"Shut up!"

"Don't even say a word! Why can't you be like Eti? Are you the first one to develop breasts that you should go about strutting chasing after boys?"

"Huh? Answer me! Are you?" she suddenly withdrew a half-raised hand to avoid slapping her sobbing daughter.

"All for what, those worthless scrawny boys," Emma's mother dejectedly rolled her eyes and stormed out banging the door behind a perturbed Emma.

Emma like most of her gang members had become fed up with regular scolding from their elders. They all considered the reproach unacceptable. They all agreed the 'Eti and Sansi' rhetoric had to end without delay.

I will skin you alive!" roared one girl's father, a fierce hunter. "And have lions kiss you."

Part of Emma's gang had curfews imposed on them, all to emulate Eti and Sansi's behaviour. That was the final stroke and the revolt was inevitable. The gang strategised an ingenious ambush against an unassuming Eti.

"One week ladies, one, is all we need to bring the flag down," Emma sneered as she concluded the strategy address meeting. All the ladies retorted in unison, some nodding whilst others whistled with faces beaming.

Indeed, it was an eventful week that lay ahead. Eti's life was unfolding into a catalogue of distress, with all sorts of depraved rumours and false witnesses testifying against her. Her father could no longer bear the disgrace and the numerous hearings at the village courtyard. To restore dignity, he just had to marry her off to her Sansirai. Well, at least they loved each other.

* * *

Mother's daughter (Cheukai)

It took me two years and 3 months to realise that I loved your father.

My stubbornness earned me a husband, and to this day, with wrinkles creeping on my face, I still possess that same spirit. Pride is what comes to mind when I recall the heights I have reached as a result of it. To get things done, at times, you have to hurt others in the process. Time heals - the wounds will heal, and eventually everyone forgets. Well, not everyone will choose to forget. The axe forgets but the tree that is cut never forgets. I wonder how many fights I would have entered had I been a boy. If I were a boy.

In my days, I was that agile woman any respectable bachelor would want to marry. Many were the advances, but I would not entertain any. Some boys wanted to test the waters only whilst others were dead serious. The whole idea reminded me of goats, how playful they were, with no intent to connect. Interesting though, one boy thought I was being the classic maiden, playing hard to get. Come to think of it, I could have married him. His name was Matamba.

It was early January when the heavens were still pouring rain for the ever-thirsty earth. Being my turn to herd cattle that day, I set off with our goats too. Something which mother had warned against, seeing the threatening storm later in the day. With my hot head I insisted on taking them. Had I known what lay ahead, I would never have left my hut that day.

The cows were calm unlike their frisky cousins, who had me running all round the meadows. That attitude was not going to deter me from herding till dusk.

In a tree nearby, a boy was watching me. Matamba. He later confessed. I could not blame him though, because my features were so striking that anyone looking at me would be entranced. It is so amazing how some people have nothing to do such that they spend an afternoon on a branch. Not to mention the cramps and discomfort, even a snake bite!

Suddenly, the azure sky was dark, covered with menacing grey clouds. Before I had gathered all the goats, large raindrops began falling. The goats went into frenzy, in a minute, they were scattered across the plain. I did not know which direction to run first. Amidst that confusion, I saw a blurry figure of a man behind some fourteen or fifteen goats. For a moment I was scared, thinking it was an apparition but, I was prepared to face whatever was coming. The man, noticing that I remained still, shouted, "Cheukai! I found your goats, it's me Matamba!"

Oh! Him! How convenient to show up at such an odd moment, playing superhero. It is not that I hated him, only his ego made me choke. He was radically chauvinistic.

With the speed of lightning, he had all my goats before me. And, eager to dismiss him, thanked him heartily, bidding farewell at the same time. He refused to leave until he saw me safely in the house. I would not hear of that. I came alone and was going to cross that river on my own again. Did he think he was a bridge!

Deep down, I knew he was right; it was too risky to cross that river single-handedly, with all that herd of animals. Someone had to coordinate and sadly, he was the only one present.

Two mornings later, I began to think he was part of our household; he was frequently in our courtyard with my father. It was his first time in our compound so; it never struck me that they were in fact, discussing me. Later, when an aunt brought the matter to my knowledge, I fumed with fury. How could I turn into a wife just like that, at the snap of a finger? Of course, every girl had to eventually go like that or otherwise, but I was not every girl. Anyway, what special qualities did Matamba have that would turn me into his wife at the blink of an eye? Despite being indebted to him, I did not want to see him, worse still, listen to him profess his undying love. Obey your elders that was a general rule. And, as such, I had to bear my aunt's order to spend an afternoon with Matamba. How depressing. That was the most boring ode I have heard to this day. I told him straight up that his heroic feat merely implied that kindness still existed. Besides, I never asked him for help.

That was the last time we spoke, he married someone else. Father was so angry that he yelled and sulked most of the time, even swore that I would never marry as I had lost my only chance of true love. He added that no one would willingly take my hand in marriage unless I dropped my awful attitude and disdainful nature. What did I care, I had all the happiness I needed.

In the main bedroom, however, mother was not happy at all. She was gravely affected and sad, fearing that I may never light a fire in my own house. The usual channel is to go through aunts, but this was too delicate for her, so she decided to confront me personally. "Cheukai my daughter, I am not forcing you to do anything against your will, I am guiding you to follow the right path. You see all these women in relationships, they are not always happy and independent, but they are bold. They make things work, one way or the other. They are stoic in the face of many challenges. More importantly, love is not based on instinct or impulse - that is not fulfilling. Some of these women were married off without willingly consenting, but with time, they have grown to love their husbands. Without a husband, you are half-human, you are not dignified. You want to be a wanderer chasing after beer parties and dances of which you never dance?" She paused for a while, waiting for an answer which never came.

Mother's voice which was initially raised had been reduced to an entreating tone. "Listen, my child, you are not getting any younger and time isn't stopping either. How many hands have you turned down? At night I lie awake pondering about your future. It is this attitude you have that has to be destroyed. And look at how you answer when we speak to you about marriage. One day you will narrate to me the ordeal which your daughter will put you through. You will run weeping to me, thinking of these very words I am saying. Your own flesh will answer back to you and without any remorse. Look at your cousins and your peers, all happily settled. If I did not know you better, I would have concluded you were hiding something. I want the best for you, do not waste your life like that. Please, my child, do this one favour for me, marry Tazivei. He will make you happy and your children will equally bring you joy. And—"

I gasped in horror, first Matamba, now Tazivei!

"Oh! Mother! Tazivei again, what does he know? After all, this is my life and it will go as I wish. I will not marry Tazivei, so don't fuss about joys of motherhood. That doesn't concern me. You must also respect my decision; I never lived your life, did I?" With that I stormed out of the hut and went to fetch water."

* * *

Thirty-six years later I look back, mother was right or, was she? Sometimes I do not know what to make of it, but it is only fair that I let go of the past and leave my Tarisai to lead her own life. That is exactly what I did back in my days. That is exactly what I did back in my days—'You only live once.

But I feel a tinge of joy when I think of my daughter's "absolute independence". Somehow it is both good and bad for her, though I am not sure in what ways. Many times, I told her that in the fullness of time it would come to pass; she would then yearn for a companion. In her mind, I was jesting; she took my words as gibberish. Her sniggering still rings fresh in my mind. Maybe she was right after all; to this day, at twenty-three, she maintains her liberty as a single lady aiming to be like the apostle Paul. Even Mother has finally accepted that her granddaughter will die a single lady, a happy one for that. Well, she has dated so there is hope she yearns for a partner. Most of her former classmates are married except for a few who run amok in search of parties.

Mother once confided in me, "You see, for some years you depressed me, but now I am glad you have a home of your own. It is Tarisai's life that is eating me up. She is so defiant that it is despicable. I have no problem with Zivai. Right now, she is in the prime of her youth, convince her to open her eyes and see reality. Otherwise, she will live a tear-stained life when she is taken by a vagabond," mother sighed, she still had more to gush out, there were a lot of pent-up emotions yet to be released.

She resumed, "I understand her father is partly to blame for this unacceptable behaviour. He is not being supportive of you; he is being wayward unlike in the days of your father. Maybe it is this technology or it is evolution. Or you call it revolution? Whatever it is, it has robbed him of his senses. Which real man would allow such nonsense to go right under his nose from a girl?" I shook my head looking up for answers.

"We were not raised like that! I tend to wander if you ever sit down with her discussing such important matters. She might be intelligent and excellent in everything else, but let me warn you, marriage is the bedrock of life. You experienced that yourself."

In no way did I intend to explain to mother that education had chiselled away some of tradition's most rooted customs. Tarisai could see the keys to her dreams matching perfectly to their lock. No key blocker would prevent the key from turning. More importantly, with her father's support, there were no drawbacks.

If it had been like that in my days, with father as my stronghold, I could have changed the course of history. In Tarisai however, I did not see history repeating itself. But, thanks to father, I am where I am today, content. In my case, mother begged me to marry Tazivei, whereas father gave mother an ultimatum.

He roared, "It's either your daughter marries by the harvest or I marry her off to Mapfumo!"

In the ensuing moments, nobody blinked, the tension was almost palpable. There was no way out apparently. At that instant, it dawned on me that I could run away and join the liberation war though rumours were saying it was nearing its end. Or rather, I could explore what those people from far away could offer, the white men who our folk were fighting against. Maybe I could start a new life, whichever way; I would embark on that adventure. We were told that when these whites, locally known as *makiwa* arrived, they preached of their God and of owning the very land which our forefathers handed down to us. There were various theories of how this position came about. History said a certain king had sold all fertile land to the whites, yet folklore said whites came with a book behind the gun.

Chapter 4

Going to the waterhole to fetch water was not only a chore. There was more to it than simply balancing calabashes on our heads. It was a parade of household skills and competence. A prospective husband could pick a wife by mere observation. The ideal wife would be one who stumbled once or not at all, who would stealthily balance her water calabash all the way without spilling even a drop. These were all signs of a hardworking woman, no one wanted a sluggish wife.

It was on one of these daily parades from the well that a friend confronted me.

She muttered, "You know friend, you may scorn love, but deep inside you it is there, fresh and unexploited. You will unravel it one day."

I made a sudden halt, aghast with disgust.

She proceeded in a murmur now, "Who are you fooling? All this virtue and hard work you display, you think it is food for the dogs? Your effort will soon pay off, they are watching you. I wish you well my friend." How could she be so naïve!

What was I supposed to say in response to that lunatic speech? I ignored her and looked at the distant fields. She interpreted my silence as a platform to elucidate.

"Stop ignoring or suppressing the feeling, let it blossom. The budding flower does not hold forever, the fullness of its beauty is when it blossoms and one fortunate bee sips its nectar. Even the flower is blissful when that happens. You will tell me one day."

All I managed to mumble was to hurry home before the herd boys caught up with us. I could have spat a lot of words at her, but I vehemently restrained myself. Such illogical conversations annoyed me to the extent that if I responded, it would offend my listeners. In the awkward silence that followed, we reached home after what seemed like an endless tour of the sacred mountains. Such a display of ignorance was quite disturbing. One did not need a ritual to open one's mind that there was more to life than marriage. Simple reasoning would clearly reveal that. But I guess common sense really is a rare gift.

That night, as I lay on my mat sad that I could not gaze at the stars anymore as the thatching had been fixed, my thoughts took me on a stroll.

The headman's son had always shown an interest in me by way of various visits to our homestead and by helping me fetch firewood in the forest. He was great fun, full of wit and handsome in a subtle way. Most of the young girls thought he was snobbish but he was merely a happy soul out to have some banter. My thoughts swept me on a serenade with the headman's son leading the way on a beautiful evening walk.

"Cheukai!"

My sleep was interrupted again. My mother, Eti, was stern that morning when she woke me. Her tone heralded bad news to me but not to others I supposed.

"You have exactly one hour to prepare yourself, your clothes and everything you own and come to the courtyard." She sharply turned before I could ask her the occasion.

It dawned on me, the inescapable had arrived. What a way to start what appeared to be a beautiful sunny day. The marriage of convenience had been finalised and to Tazivei's house it was. I gathered my few belongings and headed to the kitchen to find leftover food for I did not know when next I would eat at my new home. It's always said, one should travel on a full stomach, anything can happen.

As I was coaxing the embers, some fire started to spark. That's when it dawned on me, I could save my life by creating my own flicker by running away, that very moment without further hesitation. There was no more time to waste, no eating was necessary, I had to move immediately.

"Your husband has been arrested!" A rowdy teen stormed into the kitchen panting, halting my thoughts right away. But I wasn't married yet, I thought to myself.

"What! What happened?" I responded in shock but he had already fled the room in search of mother.

It turns out mother was in the courtyard with Tazivei's clan waiting for father to arrive and initiate the marriage proceedings.

The teen found his voice again, "It's your husband; he was taken by the police."

Rising to her feet, mother interjected, "How so, are you sure of what you are saying? My husband is a loyal and law abiding citizen. That's not possible," her voice trembled.

One of Tazivei's male relatives spoke," Child, calm down and tell us what you know. Who told you this?"

Suddenly mother recollected herself and snapped, "Ei, ei, who are you really? Huh? This is a family matter please leave or you were sent to look for fresh gossip."

"I said leave!" mother bellowed one more time and I could see the fiery Eti had come to life. She was her old self again, just as she was before marriage.

It seems she had suddenly forgotten that another family was present to forge relations with us, and it was quite disgraceful for her to speak to them like that.

One old man intervened, "Mother of Cheukai, please calm down, this is a delicate matter and if true you will need our assistance, besides, our two families were about to unite. That's why we are here isn't it? So, let's all not panic. Speak, young man."

Silence ensued as we all stood waiting for the narration. The old man ordered everyone to sit quietly.

"A-a-a-a alright, alright," the boy stuttered, "It's like this, egh,"

"Will you cut it with the funnies!" mother roared very agitated and impatient.

The boy was plainly scared. Without a word, the old wise man stomped his walking stick with authority beckoning mother to keep quiet and let the boy proceed. A handful of ants and mosquitoes were massacred in that one big thud, so much for being caught in crossfire.

He continued clearly, "He was at Chabwino Farm as per routine doing his work and he brought in a baby baboon to the boss. That's when he asked boss which of the two closely resembled the baby, a white infant or a black one. We all wanted to laugh, because you all know how they call us baboons, but boss quickly brought out his hunting gun and fired a warning shot in the air. The next moment we saw that rusty police car at the gate and they took him away on charges of insult and disrespect. That's all, and then other colleagues sent me here to report."

"Thank you, my child, you may take leave now," the old man gestured with his walking stick. All this while mother was sniffling. We had heard of many such stories of discrimination, exploitation and abuse which is why there was a war of liberation nationwide. The latest news we received was that of classified talks to end the war and that a truce was on its way. And now this! Maybe that meant the talks narrative was all a deception to make us relax and lose forever.

Dark skinned locals were labelled black and the fairer skinned ones white. How the colour bar arose was mockery as clearly no one resembled either colour to say the least. Well, that was the order of the day. Black or white.

Concurrently, I was depressed that father was in trouble and pleased that my marriage had been miraculously evaded. No sane person would continue with marital talk under such an emergency situation. All attention was diverted to organising father's release. The heavens had smiled at me. It was agreed that only males would go to the police station to plead and perhaps negotiate father's release. Mother was adamant about staying behind but she was convinced it was safer if she remained at home, due to her current infuriated temper. Just as well, she stumbled on my small bag and bruised her big toe.

She sulked, "Argh, what's this ugly bag doing here?" I stifled my giggles. "Do you go about dropping bags everywhere; have you no sense of order at all?"

In her distress she had already forgotten her stern order about packing. Mothers.

Wisdom told me that replying wasn't ideal, it would enrage her further. She couldn't sit still, she kept pacing the yard. "Some water for you mother?" I entreated. She raised her right hand authoritatively and that meant she wanted to be left alone, which I did. All I could do was to sit near her just so she felt she wasn't alone in all this. I had a myriad of thoughts, excited that I had no need to run away from home any longer as nature had rushed to my help. Instead of being a wife by end of day, I had remained free.

It was about midday when there was commotion in the yard and I momentarily panicked but ululations eased my racing mind. Rushing out, I met a crowd with father narrating his ordeal. Mother was seated meekly by his feet, grinning like a broken Congo record. She was proud of him and most villagers thought that was heroic, challenging the status quo. Father was a man of few words, so he requested for some food after which there would be a meeting with the Tazivei clan.

I wasn't concerned at all, knowing very well that it was too soon to send me away after the morning's unfortunate events. It was obviously a meeting to thank them heartily.

Indeed, father ate like a pig and gulped water almost a whole gallon. After what seemed like a lifetime due to the palpable silence, father began the meeting proceedings. Whatever was discussed initially I wasn't privy to it. However, only when I was called in did, I receive a blow.

"They facilitated my early release from jail, we can never thank them enough, my child. You have to leave today; I understand your bag is ready. They have arranged for your bride price and all is set. Be a good wife like your mother."

Without waiting for my response, the meeting was ended. Feeling helpless and defeated, I wept. Dejected, I clutched my temples, my earlier victory was short-lived.

My freedom had in a flash, slipped from my grasp. My new title was Tazivei's wife, not out of choice but out of no voice. I found myself a captive of fate's garden. An event precipitated by a white man had appeared to be a saviour but the same event had become a catalyst of my doom. Well, I had to comply with father's ruling. I was about to start my own family at the click of a finger.

* * *

Daughter, Tarisai

It all started when Tarisai was eight years old, the idea that she should never have a boyfriend. Shortly after her eighth birthday, she realised that her chest was not so flat anymore. It was slightly bumpy. Then the horror struck her, what she feared most, she was developing breasts! They had to go back, but how? Being the extensive reader that she was those days, she remembered an article about an age old practice. It mentioned that when girls grew breasts too early, an aunt would beat them with a cooking stick until they eventually vanished. The truth of that, she was about to find out. For a week she did that, nothing changed, so she resorted to plan B, slouching. That was such a bad idea because not only did it strain her neck, but it also made her look like a primate evolving to Homo Erectus and she quit that in a few days. She had to walk upright and accept that those tiny oranges were there to stay. Whether us her parents were whispering behind her back or not, she did not know, no one confronted her. That was a relief somehow because she had no idea how to explain that she was absolutely innocent. The fuss was all due to her perception and her presumed calling to ministry. She assumed that early breast development signalled promiscuity and believed they were meant for adults. Despite lacking romantic involvement, she felt threatened by this evidence and vowed never to have a boyfriend to prove her disinterest in men. She had to live up to her words and emulate Apostle Paul. For several years during her early teens, I believed that when she turned twenty-one, she would proudly look back, satisfied with the vow she made at the age of eight. Alas, what did I know; time always brings surprises. The path of being single can be rocky, but Tarisai herself shared with me that Shakespeare expressed in one of his plays the idea that those who scorn love often find themselves deeply and heavily entangled in it.

From an early age, Tarisai, knew that boys and girls become attracted to each other and eventually turn into husband and wife. However, she was not aware of the matters involved, the feelings, challenges, attitudes, reactions, heartache and joy. Knowing that so and so were boyfriend and girlfriend made her so excited that all she saw was happiness. Her cousins did not share their love escapades or would not go into much detail for fear of being reported to their parents. They agreed that she could not be trusted with such delicate information. She did not understand why her cousins made it look illegal, being secretive like that. They whispered and used code names. The mere sight of couples in a park eating, laughing and smiling at each other made her cheerful and giggly. Beautiful. Whenever she heard of a breakup, regardless of the reason, she got upset. When she asked one of her cousins the reason for breakups, she was told, "At fourteen when you have your first boyfriend, you will know why." So much for asking, not only was she disappointed by her response, but she was also panic stricken. How was she to meet the boy, what to say, what not to say and how to conduct herself. So, it was a rule everyone had to live by? What if she wasn't ready at that age? It all left her puzzled. Back in my day, at fourteen, boys and girls frisked and pottered about without any thought of dating. Indeed, this was a depraved generation.

January came and she went back to school, the only difference this time was that we threw her into boarding school. That was to be her second home, so she had to adapt and feel comfortable. She had never been exposed to such a situation of staying with a large crowd. It felt as if they were staying in army barracks, for that reason, she decided to keep a low profile minding her own business. This went on for two weeks until one night; she could not keep from eavesdropping. Her neighbours on their bunk bed were talking about a torn love note they retrieved from a bin. It had her name throughout. She was the only one with that name in her class, but the school was expansive it could be any other Tarisai. The writer wrote with a passion past the infinite of thought. Tarisai's face beamed as the girls gawked and admired the letter from her secret admirer. However, in an instant, her smile faded.

Every night she cried herself to sleep.

"O Holy Spirit you are my only friend, the only family I have right now in this desolate wilderness, in this school. A place so dry that the birds never sing," she implored daily.

* * *

Sending her to Salisbury High School boarding school was necessitated by her fixation with the leopard. Initially, her curiosity fascinated me, but it soon turned into an obsession that unsettled me. Even her father, who usually supported her, recognised the need for action before it became a compulsive obsession. I remembered one incident years ago when she was seven years old. Her answer broke my bones.

"Tarisai! Stop staring at that page and finish up your homework," I bellowed, "don't you know how to draw?"

"But I don't know what the leopard looked like before it was ripped into pieces, so I asked Jesus to draw her for me."

She glanced at me. Then turning her back to me and fixing her eyes again on her book, she finished with a smile, "So I'm waiting for him to finish."

I became annoyed with her behaviour. I expected homework to be done before supper and no excuses were welcome. And Tarisai had been seated mumbling to herself while I busied myself with cooking. What was more, that leopard troubled me. In all her school projects, Tarisai presented a leopard story and now she was asking Jesus to draw her. The little girl had concluded that the cub could have only been a female because she was so pretty it reminded her of Snow White. Despite her deep affection towards the animal, I wasn't going to let her nurture such a wrong idea of nature.

Chapter 5

It was only a matter of days before the much awaited celebrations started. The village was a hive of activity and the excitement was almost palpable. Particularly for Eti, this was an anticipated occasion. She had prepared for this day with vigour and enthusiasm only she understood. On this special gathering, they would usher into the family, their late grandfather's spirit. He would be united with his forefathers and every one of his family who went before him. From that day forth, he would be able to gather with his descended family. She knew that such ceremonies only took place between August and early October depending on the Lunar calendar. Although she had attended the preceding dance nights called *pfondas* several times, she had not been to such a ceremony. She had listened to countless narratives about these glorious ceremonies but, had not attended any.

Eight of the eldest women past childbearing age brewed beer for this gathering. The selection process was automatic, simply as detected by tradition. It states that women beyond menopause should prepare the beer in a secret location. The process started with the soaking of rapoko in the river for a week until sprouted. Once the rapoko was soaked, every night was a *pfonda*. This was all in preparation for the special day ahead. What intrigued Eti most was seeing clay pots as high as one metre simmering endlessly on a fire which lasted a week. These posts were guarded all the time. She was convinced they were safeguarding from village nuisances like Murefu. He was known to cause pandemonium and panic wherever there were crowds and food. On one incident he shouted "snake" only for all guests to flee whilst he feasted on the meat. He was purely cunning and there were several others like him.

Finally, the large beer pots were ferried from the forest to the village. There was so much fuss about the event, these were not common occurrences. Meat boiled in numerous clay pots Meat boiled in numerous clay pots, with *sadza* (a thick maize meal porridge) cooked in other pots behind the well. A lot of jostling and movement filled the backyard, with vibrant wrappers adorning those bustling about feverishly organising food preparations. Everyone had a role to play, from toddlers to the grannies.

Toddlers played with the village dogs, who eagerly attempted to snag a bone or two from the cooking pots. Meanwhile, chickens squabbled over grains and any food left over. Teens were busy collecting firewood to keep the fires alight. Grannies were constantly testing chunks of food as way of making sure the food was tasty. A group of able-bodied men were checking the drums for tightness and to ensure the best acoustics prevailed at the special gathering. All the drums had to sound perfect otherwise the ancestors would not be pleased. A wide array of instruments was on display and that's were masters would show off. *Mbira* (thumb piano) players were in their corner aiming to steal the show, whilst rattle shakers not to be overtaken, were playing high notes. With all music in place, the atmosphere was set for an enjoyable night. A few bulky men were responsible for slaughtering the bull for the feast. This night was the culmination of all the *pfonda* nights that had lasted a week, which created a memorable experience.

Ululations rose in the air. It was time. The ceremony was starting and the in-laws lay prostrate on the ground as a few elders left for the graveside to perform their formalities. A duo of drummers and a solo *mbira* player accompanied the small procession. Eti stood in amazement as she gasped at the intricate proceedings. On their return, the festivities for everyone began.

One of her notorious brothers, Mangondi, grabbed the drum as he was known for. His drumming threw everyone off their seats. No one beat the drum like he did. When his rubbery palms were hitting the tightened hide of its surface, even the air resonated in rhythm. The soil reverberated with joy as music filled the night. The atmosphere was awake and dancing in excitement. To match that unparalleled beat, beautiful voices engulfed the night air. A perfect mix of husky and velvety voices emerged under the moonlight. Dust arose in the air so intense that one could almost touch it. Men and women moved to the sound of their voices. One could see old women whose backs were crooked by day dancing with so much vigour. A beautiful rhythm rose into the air as the drums beat in unison and the much older women at once, joined in dance.

"*Toyera mudzimu dzoka, ho iye ho iye kuenda mbire, ho ho kuenda mbire* (you have gone far beyond where mortal men can reach)" harmonious music rose.

The young shy girls joined the dance floor. As they gyrated, fellow boys glared and drooled. Not only were they admiring the girls' dance moves, but they were also searching for companions. Marriage. In as much as the whole village danced the night away, Eti looked lost in thought. She had finally attended the welcoming ceremony and that's all the actualisation she yearned for.

Dancing to Eti was forbidden, she just didn't fancy it. She had grown up a reserved girl, hardly engaging in dance of any kind as her husband Sansirai could testify. He was also in attendance at the night's event. It was commonly stated that anyone who could move could dance. Well, Eti wasn't there to move, her presence was enough, still as she was. Seated throughout the night. They were celebrating their grandfather's spirit which had finally reached its destination with the ancestors. The whole party twirled to the sound of the music in such a breathtaking manner the men couldn't help but join on the dance floor. The entire yard suddenly became a dance floor as people of all ages danced and sang with the exception of Eti.

All of a sudden, she found herself at the centre of the dance floor, leaping off the ground as high as half a metre. Stunned, because no eye had seen her dance, never before, the crowd receded leaving her on the spotlight. The full moon illuminated her dance moves.

"Isn't that mother of Cheukai," some villagers whispered aghast with amazement.

Others in shock and stupefied remarked, "How can a mother jump like that, that's disdainful."

The majority were astounded and dreamily gazed at her energetic moves. Even her mean brother Mangondi skipped a beat in his drumming.

"*Chaminuka woye* (interjection expressing amusement)!" An old man shouted falling to the ground and kissing it three times. He was merely thanking the ancestors, as it appeared he had realised the significance of it all before anyone else. Soon, word was spreading amongst the amazed crowd; whispering and muttering went round that she had a spirit upon her. Hence, such dancing. When Eti stopped dancing, she was instructed to sit down and clapping amid ululations proceeded. Some village elders asked her questions as per custom.

"Who are you?" The elders' voices were reduced to a croon.

She muffled, "Little ones, I've come, I am Pfumojena."

There was silence, only the sound of drums, rattles and *mbiras* continued in low tones. The elders continued to question, "Whose child are your?"

"Jatisai," she mumbled.

"My father's totem is *Shumba Mhazi* (lion - male) from Chirimuhanzu. My father was Swarabhoy, whose father was Zuva."

More probing followed to the elders' satisfaction. The spirit upon her went on to instruct the elders on the requirements to facilitate its official welcome. Specific rites had to be performed down to the letter in order for the medium to operate at optimum efficiency. The medium had come to take care of the family.

Ululations broke accompanied by thunderous clapping. She had provided answers that they acknowledged, indicating their conviction. They had recognised who she was, rather, whose spirit was uttering through her. Eti, had officially become a spirit medium. They acknowledged that Pfumojena was Chidemo's father who in turn fathered Murambiwa, Eti's father. In short, Pfumojena was Eti's great grandfather and his spirit was now working through her. This meant a new way of life for her, whether or not it was yellow or green, she was yet to discover it all. For frowny Mangondi, sly uncle Zano and his shrewd father, this was an unwelcome development. She was proving that indeed she was destined for greatness. Instantly, their signalled at each other and sneaked off into the dead of the night.

A lot of whispering followed the near silence, "I knew there was something peculiar about her, from the time she was born I just sensed she was a great person, she is my niece you know," boasted one lady.

Not to be outdone, another one bragged, "That's why we named her Eti. Did you know she's the only one with that name, and she is my in-law?" Stifled laughter followed as the whole village knew the story around Eti's unique name, and it was all from a dream by her father.

When quiet Eti had regained herself, an old lady recounted to her what had transpired, from how she leaped onto the dance floor to the arrival of Pfumojena. This was her call, chosen by the ancestors and she had to accept it or otherwise.

Chapter 6

After an invigorating night of activity, the stillness that ensued the next day was almost palpable. It turned out the previous night's revellers had exhausted all their energy on the dance floor and indulging in beer. Yards were hardly swept and no one seemed to be in the mood for carrying out any chores. Empty clay pots lay around the host's kitchen and the in-laws were expected to clear all the dirt. How unfair.

"Who is fetching water ladies? Last time I did, there are so many dishes today, our backs will break."

"We are just as good as donkeys, so much for being married huh!" The daughters-in-law sulked and grumbled as their got on with the housework.

Without looking up, Mangondi's wife waved a dish of murky water, laden with last night's leftovers, towards him.

"Watch it, stupid woman! Is that how you bath where you come from!"

Instantly she fell on her knees almost lying prostrate and apologised to her angry husband. That was a total mistake. Although Mangondi never hit anyone with his bare hands, he straightened with his hippo belt. A belt he wove when he was eighteen after he skinned a hippo along the shores of the river Mara. Legend said he killed it with a small axe, *gano*. His wife pleaded with him not to unleash the wrath of his belt later at night. As in the past, he used it while she slept, around midnight when she least expected a beating. Just one leash and he stored it away. She respected him more out of fear of the belt than love for her husband. That is one possession whose relevance she never understood, especially in their house and marriage. To him, it highlighted his prowess, how he single-handedly defended himself and killed a ferocious hippo. He still adored it the same way he did when he made it forty-three years ago. It solidified his manliness. Sometimes he carried it on his shoulder like an epaulette went he went drumming or drinking.

"Father of my kids, the broad roof over my head, you know I could never disrespect you like that. Ple-e-e-ease forgive my stu-stupidity. I will never do it again. I should have first—" Mangondi stormed off, kicking a bucket half full of water. As expected, the eldest sister-in-law in the clan raised her hand beckoning the terrified woman to follow her husband. She had wanted to be relieved of her duties but not through such a frightening incident. Mangondi when irate was like a wounded lion. She found him pacing about the room, eyes bulged, almost popping out.

"Kneel…" he snarled with fists clenched, "keep pushing me and I will finally get that girlfriend you so much suspect I have." She lowered her head further.

"Such humiliation. Were you thinking at all?" Silence was her best defence against his rumble. She learned to tolerate his roughness, much as she did with his infamous charm, mastering the art of neutralising his wrath.

She had long suspected him of infidelity because of his popularity in drumming. Many women of different ages admired Mangondi and wished they could marry him or at least spend an afternoon with him. He seemed to enjoy the attention despite being married. Even the white farmer's wife was rumoured to fancy him.

A hurried knock saved her. The family had been summoned to the courtyard on account of last night's development where Eti had received a special call. It was not an event to dismiss. Someone had to relate to Eti the proceedings of the night and a ceremony arranged to welcome the spirit medium. For a long time Eti was known for weaving spectacular baskets, her neatness and trademark '*e*' added an undeniable appeal to her crafts. Villagers from beyond the plain, as far as Gurumombe, travelled long distances to buy her baskets. She had begun conducting free classes as a way of giving back to the community that had admired her since her maiden days. Emma, her nemesis, attended classes during the first two weeks the training started. Most people claimed she had a sinister plan up her sleeve, probably to steal Eti's secret formula or to cast a spell on her so she loses customers and students. Whatever her intentions were, time would tell, it always does. Eti didn't care; she had better and bigger dreams than chasing petty issues like Emma. Almost all the time Emma frowned and spoke rudely. She was quite unpopular with the villagers. She was mean, and it showed well on her face, worsened by numerous mosquito bites, resembling a polka dot pattern. Despite plotting against Eti, she ended up with a lanky, lazy husband who, though faithful, was ultimately a good-for-nothing man. He only basked in the sun and followed beer parties. Some said he was a spy for the white army and that's how he earned a living. At one point during a verbal fight with his enraged wife, she revealed his feigned sluggishness was a calculated act. Surprisingly, he seemed to keep his family well provided for, they had enough food on the table, even eating the choicest meat available. All this pointed to him working as a spy against his own kinsmen. Most villagers disliked him and openly agreed it was all disguise, that basking habit of his, he would be gathering information about basically everyone.

An early morning meeting meant the elders were in a hurry. As usual, the men sat on stools to symbolise their high status in society and the women sat on the earth to show their humility and low social standing. Even their voices had to remain low. The meeting was chaired by a whitehaired man in his early nineties. All he knew was that he was born in the year of the locusts which was an appropriate estimate to place him in that age group. This nonagenarian was the chief's special and most senior advisor who spent his day napping in his yard. Today, however, his presence was necessitated by the inevitable call of Eti. He admitted that he longed to see this day, then he would be happy to meet his ancestors.

As the night's events were recounted, Eti's eyes widened, and she shuddered. She leaned forward, tense with anticipation, scanning her elders' faces for any signs. Her gaze darted around trying to see if she could pick any answers from the querying eyes. It was not surprising that some family members could not understand why the ancestors had chosen her, what it is that set her apart to be worthy of such a demanding calling. Maybe it was just fate. All she wanted was a peaceful life, showcasing her creativity through making baskets. What started as a pastime became a source of income. She had the least, if not zero, interest in this development. The few attendees at the meeting whispered and muttered. Obviously, the jealous ones sulked and wished they were the rightful recipients of this calling. In her early years a group of envious girls plotted against her and now again she was the subject of envy. Not only from Emma, but her brother and uncles were vying for her downfall. It was not rare to have such rivalry between families, but your own siblings that was another level of hatred. It was pure cruelty. Two camps of haters emerged at the meeting, one openly displayed their dislike whilst another was subtle.

Mangondi was the first to declare that it was probably a mistake by the ancestors to select Eti. He claimed he dreamt several times that he carried with him a special spirit, and he was convinced this was it. He spoke about it at every opportunity he got. Even the kids knew his mantra, *"pane dare guru riri pandiri* (there is a great spiritual calling upon me)."

"That's insane Mangondi! How ridiculous can you get? Everyone here knows the dictates of our tradition," the advisor exclaimed. Seemingly absent minded, the rickety old man gathered phlegm and it landed near the headman's right shoe. Muffled chuckling spread across the yard, it was the headman, and one couldn't openly laugh at him for fear of punishment and victimisation. One outspoken woman, Sharai, who had a known vendetta with the headman, broke into laughter. Clapping her hands, she remarked, "Oh yes!" All eyes looked at her blankly yet no one dared to comment. She had for long accused him of misappropriation of land in favour of whites and for favouritism. Nonetheless, she lacked sufficient evidence to implicate him at the chief's court.

As if by instinct, the headman looked at the substance that lay at his feet. His eyes met with thick, course yellowish-grey slime. Abruptly, he slung his arm down and covered it with some soil. Then, he plunged it into his trousers' pocket, retrieving a shiny handkerchief whose threading was starting to show. Scrambling to his feet, he handed it to the old man. For a moment I hoped that a fight would erupt with the headman grabbing him by the collar tearing one button off his worn-out viscose shirt. But, no, it was all peace and quiet. I didn't quite understand the headman it times; he was an odd character.

Out of the blue, the wise old man began to sneeze uncontrollably, losing his balance in the process. The rickety man landed on his bottom. Rubbing his behind, he regretted keeping stones in his back pockets. He had a habit of eating little stones. He claimed it brought him luck. But surely, after the day's events, he would never pick stones, whether big or small. It was now impossible that the meeting would continue as one by one, the attendees left starting with Sharai. Meanwhile, the headman and two older women attended to the old man.

Eti remained there, dumbfounded. She whispered to her husband that the entire disturbance was a sign it wasn't her fate to be a spirit medium. "It can only be confirmation," she mumbled.

"Phew, what just happened?"

"What can all this mean?"

Whenever she felt bewildered, Eti went to a lonely place on the banks of the River Mara. There, she would throw three stones in one go, then two, and finally one. Immediately afterwards, she began to read and count the ripples emerging in the water, trying to trace and predict their direction. In the midst of this activity, she said her thoughts calmed, and like a whiff of air, she recollected herself, finding peace once again. This tradition started way back during her courtship with Sansirai. They shared even toothbrushes. That was ridiculous but their house, their rules, "one family one tooth," was their motto. Happy moments, sad moments and this was their hideout when all seemed senseless. Events of the morning may have made her long for this magical place to gather her thoughts from. She just had to go. It was their place of solace, their happy place. Despite her size, Eti remained active and unburdened by her body weight. Hence, she ran toward the river with such speed that dust filled the air. While still moving at full speed, a hand intercepted her, pulling and bringing her to a halt. Instantaneously, she was drawn into an embrace, realising it was her husband. All he did was hug her tightly as she repressed sobs.

"For the first time in my life, I don't know what to do." Sansirai held her closer as she murmured.

"I don't. I just don't." She said, speaking between sobs.

"You will come out good, my dear wife, I know you will"

Eti hadn't broken down like this since settling with Sansirai twenty five years ago in the remarkable year 1953, the days leading to her rushed marriage. She had a conviction that as long as Sansi was her support system, she could stand. On her own she was brave and resilient, but she needed that support which her husband knew exactly how to provide.

Her husband narrated to her all the previous night's events and when she took a long deep breath, he stopped. He knew her too well to know what that signalled.

"So, I have to let go of my dreams and start a new life? You know I never anticipated this, it wasn't in our plans too. How do I just wake up a different person? A new life, a new road. Without prior consultation, even in a dream or something. What an unpleasant surprise."

Holding her hand gently, he let her speak her heart out uninterrupted.

"Listen Eti, remember your name and how it came about? The signs were there but you may have ignored them. It doesn't just happen." She forced a smile while shrugging.

"Was it not by way of a special instruction? You are not ordinary. This is your new life my beloved. Something massive like this was meant to happen, just that we didn't know when. I am happy for you. The ancestors chose you from the beginning of time, and no one can change that."

He squeezed her hand and said, "Understood?"

"What if I don't want, you know what sweetheart, I don't want. And that's final" She sharply turned her head sideways, looking far from him as possible.

"You have to want. If you were part of the decision making you would have been consulted, okay. Let it be. Today's meeting was not to ask for your consent, it was to inform you and enquire about preparations for your appointment. You are merely an accessory, a vessel. I am here for you all the way." Eti's face drooped and her eyes appeared to recede.

"Do you know that you are lucky you were not tormented by sickness? Your calling was direct and straightforward."

Others are ravished with plagues and so much misfortune that they relinquish the day they were born. Check what happened with the late headman. Although he died of malaria, he had gone through a spat of mysterious diseases. Even the herbalist couldn't cure him until that spirit medium revealed his calling. So, you see..."

Eti let her head hang loosely on his shoulder in dejection. "Okay, I'll go along with it. Let's go."

The journey back home was a silent one with occasional holding of hands. It was a ten-minute walk but as they trudged on, it took double that time. At last, they reached the courtyard, only to find it packed as in the morning. The group had assembled again to finalise the morning's disrupted discussions. The headman sat on the highest stool as usual marking his authority. Unlike the murmuring and laughing earlier, this time everyone was quiet and attentive like small geese. Even the rickety advisor sat fit as a fiddle.

The headman stood and scanned around feigning a menacing look, which his nose forbade as it had that pointy end with a bulge on the left and a sudden slide towards the mouth. Whenever he scowled, he ended up with a grinning face instead. And instantly, his audience would giggle. He sternly eyed the rickety man as he opened the session.

"Greetings to you all, I will go straight to the point as we have many errands to do, the sun is already overhead."

"I will be as brief as possible and won't tolerate any form of disturbance," he retorted eyes fixed on Sharai.

"Mother of Cheukai, I'm here both as your headman and as your uncle…obviously you are elated with this development. The next stage is to invoke the medium to direct us how to plan for your welcome and do what we have always known to do. All ceremonies are different in that the medium has to specifically instruct what they prefer and how they want it done, hence we cannot overlook this and the sooner we do it, the better for everyone, including the medium."

The silence was broken by the headman's continuation.

"Maybe you have seen others going through the same path as you are now, but without much understanding. You were a bystander, now you join that walk."

All this while, Eti yawned continuously, the intensity of her yawning growing with each passing moment. Unknown to Eti, yawning signified the arrival of Pfumojena. It was common for spirit mediums to yawn, a subtle signal that those in the know would pay attention to. However, despite her persistent gaping, no one noticed.

"Your father is here and you know why he named you Eti, he was—," a roar terrified the headman who lost balance and staggered a few steps. Chuckling, ululating, and clapping spread across the yard.

"Roarrrr, iyoooooooo, iyoooooooooo, roarrrr."

Ululations and clapping accompanied the roaring and all eyes went in Eti's direction as she continued roaring. They ululated to acknowledge the legitimacy of the spirit upon her as well as its presence. A cup of water was passed around the yard and given to Eti whilst the crowd greeted the man within her.

"Greetings great ancestor, how is it where you are coming from?"

"My children, greetings"

"These are the items of my vocation. I want a white fabric, black fabric in the following dimensions..." she roared and resumed instructing them.

At this time, even her father and all the old men subordinate to her. After all, Pfumojena was older than them all. He had to be respected. Similarly, the body through which he was speaking commanded equal respect, for it carried a great man.

"...I will only use snuff made by men and..."

"To finish off before I go, the ceremony will be done within two weeks from today, and the beer has to prepared starting today at sunset."

After the crowd had exhausted all their questions, Eti roared again and quivered before bowing in silence. The women ululated whilst the men clapped hands in appreciation of the great ancestor's presence and speech. It was as if she had exerted all her energy and needed to be rejuvenated.

Well, at last, the meeting finished without hiccups. Someone had to relay the proceedings of the meeting to Eti. She couldn't join the preparation team as it was her event, she was the host.

The buzz in Eti's homestead began with the specific beer preparation being monitored by the old wise women. All the intricacies had to be precise. The task of finding the required material was assigned to Mangondi, which was a bad decision given that he disliked anything extraordinary about his sister. He openly said he wished she lived a mediocre life. All the grandeur was his; he was the first child, male at that. It was a common misconception that male first children were the apple of their parents' eyes. They were leaders of their lineage and a female first child wasn't considered head of the family. She was of no significance. Her duties were domestic and making the matrimonial home habitable. Nothing more and nothing less. Initially, I thought I could fight the system, but I gave in too early. I didn't want to cause unnecessary stress to my mother, Eti; father had pressured her enough concerning my marriage. It was only prudent to let life be and follow the tide. That's how I married Tazivei.

* * *

On his way to buy the fabric, Mangondi passed by the farmer's house to ask for referrals to find inexpensive yet quality markets. The farmer's wife, Nancy was quick to stop him at the gate. Mangondi's temper made him repulsive and the farmer openly hated him and Nancy avoided any altercation. Thus, she went to intercept him far from the house. Besides, she didn't want any suspicions raised between her and the attractive adept drummer. Not on her doorstep at least. Each time she followed his drumming, it wasn't purely for the love of music, but the attraction she felt for him, they were drawn to each other. This was not heard off during that era. It was taboo, crossing enemy lines. Sleeping with the enemy was as good as treason, sell-outs were not tolerated on either side of the colour spectrum. That was betrayal at its worst.

She grabbed him by the elbow almost knocking him off balance, "You-u-u what are you doing here? Are you out of your mind?"

"He is home, he will shoot you," he laid a dirty index finger on her lips, silencing her.

"Relax sweetness, I know I miss you but I'm not that daft. Now listen, I just need to ask your esteemed Jack where to buy good fabric, I know he often goes to town." Nancy's tense posture softened as she took a deep breath, her shoulders dropping slightly as a faint smile played on her lips.

"Is he home?"

She took another long deep breath, running her lean fingers through her glistening brunette hair, revealing a ruby studded wedding ring as the sun shone on it. Until recently, she had kept her hair blonde and that's how even her husband liked it. Then one day, she wore a floral burgundy dress with a sweetheart neckline which really gave out a perfect silhouette it got even the headman commenting. From that day she tinted her hair brunette, the headman had exclaimed that shade would enhance her beauty just as the dress did. Who wouldn't be happy with a compliment, she tried it out and she liked it much to her husband's annoyance who she replied, "You are welcome not to look at me you know."

"Come this way Sir." Mangondi ogled at her.

"Wait there, don't step on the veranda,' she bawled at him frowning yet winking.

"He's coming and he'll see you out." Turning her back toward Mangondi, she sashayed off with her skirt revealing a long glowing leg. Mangondi feeling helpless he couldn't flirt with her, kicked some stones and bruised his big toe.

"Hey John, what can I do for you?"

Mangondi clenched his fist at this uncouth greeting. 'John' or 'boy' was a common name given to any native male person by the whites. They did not bother knowing one by their real name, well one line of thought was that native names were complex and difficult to pronounce. Imagine calling M-a-n-g-o-n-d-i. Others said it was a display of pride, arrogance, exploitation and oppression. That equated to stripping someone of their identity.

Without enduring further irritation, the drummer quickly narrated his request. He got the directions and hurried away, straight to town. Mangondi crafty as he was, had come to see Jack because he knew the farmer was involved in some unscrupulous merchant deals. He was in the trade of buying rejects and selling them at the full price instead of a discounted price and somehow Mangondi had found out and he threatened to report Jack to the police with evidence. The farmer dreaded receiving a negative report, especially since many of his clients were police officers themselves. If it weren't for the fact that these officers were his customers, he wouldn't have cared where Mangondi reported. However, he had earned their trust and secured his market, making it imperative for him not to lose them. This was Mangondi's secret weapon, something he kept hidden even from his mistress. Mangondi confided in his cronies, revealing his plan to purchase fabric that would quickly wear out, causing Eti to repeatedly spend money replacing them after only a few washes. The cloth he intended to buy ran off easily and wasn't flame retardant. He would exploit that texture characteristic at a later date. His uncles were also involved in this plan.

He hurried to buy the material, pretending to be happy for his sister and to show his full support for her, especially during this significant event. Still, his parents were doubtful of him, having been around long enough to not be fooled by his actions. They regarded him with scepticism.

Returning from town, he quickened his pace, shoulders slumped, a subtle air of disappointment clinging to him like a shadow. He veered off his usual path, drawn instead toward the familiar brick facade of the school where Nancy worked. Though it was a detour, every step was justified by his affection for Nancy. The adage says forbidden waters are always sweet.

As he walked, a tension hung in the air, palpable in the way his gaze darted nervously from side to side, as if fearing discovery. The mere notion of glimpsing Nancy in secret seemed to fuel his steps, adding a quiet urgency to his stride.

Finally, the schoolyard gates came into view, and with them, the sight of Nancy amidst a sea of young faces. She stood tall and poised, her presence commanding attention without effort. They were like two love-struck teenagers falling in love for the first time. Maybe that was infatuation. They both new they were taking big risks particularly for Mangondi. He knew he could even face a prison sentence. Although he loved her, she wasn't worth a prison term for. It was his habit to pop in at the school unannounced just so they talk briefly. That was enough for daytime escapades. Being a teacher, it wasn't odd for her to interact with people of all ages, hence no suspicions were raised. Even on this day when she was with the headman. After all, the headman's son Tikana was her student, it could be parent-teacher consultation.

The headman held Nancy's palm as if he were a palm reader, while the two chatted, unaware of Mangondi peeping through the window. He budged in on them just as Nancy aggressively pulled her hand away.

"So, as I was saying, the boy needs a genteel approach, don't be too harsh on him otherwise he will fail. Okay." The teacher, Nancy explained.

That statement was enough to dismiss the headman as the teacher greeted the visitor in as professional a manner as possible. She played her cards well.

As the men crossed, the drummer turned sideways hiding a menacing look as he greeted the headman out of formality. Mangondi scowled like someone ready to push and pounce on him.

Nancy, noticing the one-sided animosity, banged the door and swiftly turned to Mangondi, her cheeks flushed red.

"Now let me remind you something, drummer-boy," she continued with teeth gritted.

"I am Jack's wife, I am a teacher and meeting the public is what I do. You can't complain. Besides what do you know about pedagogy, huh?"

An unexpected outburst from a lover pierces the heart, creating a hole of anger.

"Woman, listen, that's not what I saw, you—" he began, but she snapped at him midway through his sentence.

"Leave my classroom now. Get out!"

Instantly, with shoulders slumped and head bowed down, he trudged outside. Suddenly the bag with the fabric weighed down on his shoulders. He even noticed his sore toe. What love can do to a man. As he dragged himself home, he kicked himself several times for loving such an arrogant woman. The drummer knew too well that if he lingered, he could end up beating her and the consequences were unimaginable. Mangondi waddled as the seemingly short journey lugged on. The trip that should have taken a kilometre seemed to stretch into an eternity as Mangondi trudged on. Uncle Zano waved at him, but his vacant stare revealed his distraction. He only regained his senses after hitting the gate. Women!

He reached the family courtyard and ululations welcomed him as older women ran to collect the plastic bag with fabric. This signalled progress, everything seemed to be moving smoothly, the beer preparations were underway already. A young boy ran to summon Eti for she lived some hundreds of metres away at her husband's family yard. Her in-laws understood she had this newly found duty form her paternal home and they supported her. Other in-laws could have objected, claiming a daughter in-law knew her place and that was the kitchen, bearing children only and keeping the home tidy. It was a privilege to have that freedom.

Before Eti's arrival, Mangondi acted fast to avoid anyone from examining the fabric and asking questions.

"You know kids and scissors, let me put this special cloth away," he said locking the cupboard and standing in front of it. Blocking everyone's view. the ordinarily big kitchen seemed small as a crowd gathered for the fabric.

Chaos ensued. Everyone was eager to hold the cloth and connect with it. Eti had to see it too.

"Eish, no one cares about how I fared. It was a difficult journey marred with mishaps." He narrated a sob story such that his audience gasped and pitied him.

Chapter 7

My mother Eti was old enough to make her own decisions, she had the experience of time, whereas Tarisai struggled with her emotions and convictions. She lacked emotional intelligence. Self-awareness is critical to discernment, which is why one can ramble if they want. Nonetheless, Tarisai excelled in her studies and she had an eye for mathematics with an inclination towards engineering. She pestered anyone who could listen with her favourite math concepts, but her true calling lay in another subject.

Since her childhood, she claimed she was called. I remained neutral and didn't have much knowledge on the subject matter, hence I couldn't advise much. I hoped her grandmother Eti would convince her otherwise. Throughout her childhood, she had focused on her calling, the leopard story, and nothing more. So, when she developed a keen interest in math, I encouraged her like an enthusiastic fan. That way, I diverted her attention, hoping she could lead a normal life. Her bike brought relief to my worries. In her final year of primary school, she came top of her stream and received a bicycle on prize giving day. The villagers laughed, saying the bike once belonged to the headmaster's son, and when he got a new one, they donated it to the school. They could jest all they wanted, but I was glad my daughter could enjoy a normal pastime riding across the valley. Apart from that, she spent her time reading, drawing, writing, strolling at along forest's edge or cracking nuts with my mother.

Our houses were clustered, all situated on the bounds of the in-laws' land. A common proverb, *'rooranai vematongo'* (marry locally), reinforced the practice of marrying within the vicinity, ensuring familiarity and security. This tradition also helped to avoid marrying a criminal or someone whose background was unfamiliar. However, it's worth noting that not all marriages were free from such risks; good girls sometimes fell for bad boys. The elders were correct when they said where they are hit the hardest is where they run to. Tarisai told me that nowadays they call it Stockholm Syndrome. Anyway, families lived communally, sharing almost everything. So, it was routine for me to send Tarisai to my mother's house, where her sister Zivai socialised daily with my young brothers.

The midwife had scolded my mother for the wide gap between her children. Although I was already married, my younger brother was still in early adolescence. Tarisai disliked him because of their frequent religious arguments. Despite her kindness, Tarisai was bossy and conceited, perhaps due to her inquisitive nature. Stubbornness was another trademark of hers, leading to complaints from her teachers. A learning environment thrives in the absence of stubbornness. It's important for these young ones to understand that.

Fortunately, Tarisai grew up to be a beautiful dainty lady with protruding eyes and a long heart-shaped face. Her grandpa, a man of humour, described hare face as resembling a duiker (*huso hwemhembwe*). The day Tarisai saw a duiker in the forest, she sulked for a week. The more she sulked, the more everyone giggled. One day she burst in laughing and that ended her grumbling. Well, Tarisai and Zivai were all grown now I didn't want to herd them like cattle. I let them be. I had even let Zivai choose her husband with minimal interference. May his soul rest in peace.

Sometimes I reminisce those days preceding her marriage. Zivai dated a carpenter and they exchanged clothes as a sign of their commitment. Tarisai mocked them saying, "He just wants a decent dress to give his sister. Will that dress stop him from marrying someone else, and his sweater stop you? Come on, don't be naïve. Adults can behave like kids sometimes," she rolled her eyes.

Nowadays the man gives the girl a ring on their engagement day but others go straight for the customary marriage and skip all other western nuances. Seeing the possible tension, I chimed in, "Girls you remember *musengabere* (marriage by prearranging to carry a woman you are in love with to your homestead, similar to abduction.) I am glad the days of *musengabere* are over otherwise skinny men like your father would never have married if that was the only way to marry. Girls you know literally it means 'to carry a hyena and run away with it.' Some of us were pigs not hyenas. I may have been too heavy for him. That one was for petite girls like you Tari." The girls broke into laughter.

Zivai wasn't offended and she didn't want to argue with her; all she said was, "Tarisai, Tarisai, Tarisai," shaking her head.

"I'm getting married the Saturday before grandma's ceremony, you know that, right. I implore you, please don't blabber during the proceedings. Do not ruin my day."

She fiddled with Tarisai's cheek and left the room. Tarisai felt insulted, but, well, she couldn't always have everything her way. Zivai rarely objected to traditional beliefs and complied happily almost all the time. She was grounded in customs, whilst Tarisai questioned everything.

Zivai popped her head in at the door, "I almost forgot, could you ask the God you believe in to bless my day and marriage. I won't tolerate any nuisances." As Tarisai was responding, Zivai vanished.

Tarisai paced about the lonely room biting her lower lip and fuming. She jumped onto the bed, face down and covered her head with a pillow. Taking in the fragrance of soap from the recently washed pillowcase, she dozed off.

* * *

Zivai's marriage proceedings had all proceeded well with no hiccups. I feared a few drunk uncles would create drama especially uncle Zano, but no. Even Tarisai behaved. She watched all the steps without asking any questions, this being her first attendance, I'd thought she would talk endlessly. Wonders do happen indeed. My mother and I beamed with joy after witnessing Zivai's marriage. What a fruitful day.

It is sad that we cannot journey ahead in time to flip the pages of our lives. Only those who have gone before us, ahead of time, can see what we cannot see—our ancestor. If only we had known that Zivai's marriage would be short-lived, we would have left her pages unwritten. But that is our way, everyone.

* * *

Today, the village bustled with preparations for my mother's ceremony, but things began on the wrong footing. Almost everyone was anxious. Beer and snuff checks had passed the night before and again in the morning, yet the worry stemmed from the absence of the fabric needed for the ceremony. Mangondi, who held the key to the wood and glass cupboard where the fabric was stored, was nowhere to be found, and his wife had no knowledge of his whereabouts. Breaking the glass meant Eti's path would be marred with much misery as numerous as the broken pieces. That wasn't an option, neither was breaking the wood. Dismantling it meant Eti would soon rescind her call as she would prove to be weak for it. Purchasing new fabric seemed plausible, but Mangondi had encountered serious problems on his trip to town, and even the sellers had troubled him, making it risky to send someone inexperienced. Without this material, the ceremony could not proceed, and there was no ample time to rectify the situation. There was no ample time as everything had to be in place well in advance, especially the fabric that Eti needed to see. The elders of the family needed to see all essentials for the ceremony and dedicate them. The event was set to start after two in the afternoon towards dusk and would continue till daybreak, but this bad start signalled gloom. Eti bit her nails, fumbling on her bed and fidgeting the whole time. She kept asking people, "Is he back?" The same answer pushed her back on the bed. She murmured, "Maybe it's all pointing to one thing. I should quit and continue with my mundane life. This is certainly a wrong move; this path isn't meant for me. Now I can see my brother was right; this should be his, not mine. It's not too late to opt out. Besides, I never chose this.

Will my husband think I'm a failure, and my parents too? Will my kids still look up to me if I quit before starting because of setbacks? Is this what you, my ancestors, called me for, to be the village's fool? A coward?" she asked, looking at the sun through the window. Perplexed eyes looked down, and one woman held her hand.

Her support system, Sansi, gathered in the courtyard with the village elders, discussing possible implications and solutions. The mater had to be resolved fast. Otherwise, it could be a bad omen equally for everyone, not just Eti. Uncle Zano's father sneaked off from the meeting in the pretext of going to the restroom. Instead, he knocked at Eti's door. Startled, she ushered him in. The women attending to Eti looked at one another with questioning eyes.

"My child, don't blame yourself. None of this is your fault. Entering this road would be a false move. It's a thorny path, fraught with pitfalls and perils, as you can see. These are clear signs. Be wise and avoid this impending demise." All the while he looked down hiding a sly smile. However, Eti, with her strong emotional intelligence, may have sensed the feigned sincerity behind his words. While others might attribute it to the influence of the great spirit, she saw through people like glass.

"Anyway, you will be fine. When you are ready, send someone to Mbuya Zano. Be well," he said, now looking at her. Mbuya Zano was his wife, and to any sane person, one would wonder why a fox would be kind to a goat. With that, he left. Eti shook her head three times, starting from the left. This confirmed her inclinations towards him. When she shook her head starting from right that, would confirm good intentions. She always shook her head exactly three times, and only more when under a trance, and that signified noth-ing. The women in waiting again eyed each other, hiding muffled chuckles. They erupted into laughter, exchanging high fives as they jeered. Eti couldn't resist joining in, a smile forming on her face. Everyone had that man's intention fig-ured out. His words revived Eti. She knew what to do and she'd do it. Ordinarily, she would have sought solace and ideas by the river, but not in this instance. That day, it was about the power of one's own mind; it wasn't about the river but about perspective. She was strong on her own. To flee or to fight, that was the question. Gathering the ladies in her hut, she shared her plan with them. They all nodded. She sought their opinions to craft a foolproof plan, not just to receive mere agreements. The beaming smiles encouraged and reassured her that she was making the right decision. As she walked out with her head held high, a hand pulled her back.

"Is there a problem?"

"No, no, not at all, Eti, it's just… it's—"

Eti lowered her head and her eyes followed suit. "It's just that we are honoured that you considered us lowly people and asked for our advice. All the best."

The others echoed the same sentiments. Eti then hugged the woman who held her and left.

* * *

Eti rushed to the kitchen, ordering the kids to play outside. They stood there staring at her and she handed them a morsel of bread so they would go outside. Left alone, she set to work. Sharp as ever, Eti remembered her brother hiding a spare key in the thatching at the beam farthest from the door. He hid it so he could steal whatever he fancied from the cupboard without arousing suspicion, as he had led everyone to believe there was only one key. Eti hoped to catch him red-handed one day, which is why she didn't report or remove the key. She fetched the key, retrieved her fabric, replaced the plastic, and fluffed it up. Satisfied, she returned the key and left as quickly as she had entered. Everything seemed undisturbed. Once in her room, she examined the fabric, and with one glance, it was evident to everyone that it was of the lowest quality possible. It would be a miracle if it lasted the night. That wretched Mangondi!

In the courtyard, the men's efforts were futile. A team was dispatched to search for Mangondi in the neighbouring villages, as his drumming often took him across different settlements. News spread rapidly that he was being sought after. Meanwhile, he relaxed in Uncle Zano's father's house, enjoying the panic and escalating drama. The climax promised to be grand, and he intended to make a dramatic entrance. He sipped his beer with impunity, seemingly unfazed by the chaos unfolding around him.

Outside the elders decided to postpone Eti's ceremony, but they hadn't informed her. Uncle Zano's father headed to Eti's hut to enquire about her decision. He met Ems halfway through the courtyard. "It's you my child, how wonderful," he forced a smile. "Have you talked to Mbuya Zano? Your decision awaits and time has run out."

"It's sad father, lets discuss in the courtyard."

He was puzzled but refrained from asking anything as Eti walked with a scowl on her face. She briskly led the way, with Uncle Zano's father trailing behind, until they reached the courtyard.

Upon exchanging greetings, she spoke up, "My elders, lets proceed as planned. Let the drumming begin."

Confused men exchanged looks and waved their hands, bombarding Eti with questions. She responded with just two words, signalling to a friend to take over the announcements before she went back to get ready. Just then, Mangondi showed up, staggering and clutching a beer. The men erupted in chaos, some shaking him, others slapping him, demanding to know where he had been. Too drunk to answer, he simply pointed to the east, guffawing as his head bobbed. Realising he couldn't provide any answers, the crowd let him go, deciding to deal with him later. They had more pressing matters to attend to; he wasn't the centre of attention after all and couldn't steal the limelight. His father sternly warned him and pushed him aside, "I will not forget this easily."

The final preparations were complete. An anxious crowd paced the courtyard, whispering about the likelihood of success for the day's event. Anything seemed possible after Mangondi's earlier feat. Curiosity grew as no updates were given on how it would all proceed. The villagers had a habit of grouping and gossiping about almost every topic imaginable, from anthills to new wives and mischievous herd boys. Though reserved, Eti wasn't to be underestimated; she was intelligent. Though she was a lamb by nature, she could transform into a lion when provoked.

Chapter 8

All drums had been tuned to perfection, the music was set, and the festivities commenced. The echoes and reverberations followed each drum beat and in turn matching the rising excitement of the singing crowd. Initially, only a few tipsy individuals were scattered around the yard, but soon more joined in the celebration. Clad in uniform brown shirts, the *mbira* players began with low tones, syncing perfectly with the drums. Not to be outdone, the rattlers joined in, adding to the beauty of the accompaniment.

Old men nodded in unison to the rich music which was so vibrant that even the trees swayed in rhythm. The melodies drew chiefs from villages afar, while the singers mesmerized the crowd with their carefully curated songs. Everything fell into place like a tapestry in the making; would Eti's entrance be the final stroke to complete the painting? Amidst the excited crowd, there were also those indifferent to the festivities. From an early age, I learned that not everyone shares in your happiness; there are always those who secretly hope for things to go awry, providing them with juicy news to discuss. Simple minds discuss people, while great minds figure out ways to improve their situations. Everything was arranged to the last detail, except for the fabric, which people were unsure about. Eti had convinced them that the program would not change under any circumstances, except perhaps in the event of her death, which she didn't foresee happening on this special day—it just had to happen.

The dancers needed more space to move freely; they danced as if they were trying to navigate their way out of a crowded bus. Finally, a few people were selected to join Eti inside the hut, which had been decorated for the event. Eti roared and shook vigorously, and ululations and clapping arose. Meanwhile, the music continued outside. Eti had chosen a woman almost my age to be her assistant, someone who would also translate or relay messages when they weren't clear. This choice seemed natural, as Eti had been her mentor for a long time, and she had almost learnt the weaving trade from her.

The proceedings succeeded as Pfumojena came upon Eti and spoke a few important words, to which everyone in the hut nodded and applauded. All the while, Eti took the first pinch of snuff and passed it around so everyone could take a sniff. Some, not accustomed to it, sneezed continuously. Despite being new to it, Eti seemed like a professional, having inhaled it a few times in the preceding weeks. People wanted to ask about the fabric, but that would be an insult to Pfumojena; his arrival implied that everything was done correctly.

The solemnities of the event forbade people from having private conversations in the hut. Wonder and amazement was written on their faces. Uncle Zano's father drooped in an instant, beads of sweat covering his broad forehead. Betrayal. He sulked and mumbled about whether they had perhaps sent a boy to do a man's job. Perhaps Mangondi had felt sorry for his sibling that he opted out. This task was not for cowards. I bet the old man couldn't wait to leave the hut and confront Mangondi, intending to hold him accountable and nip insolence in the bud.

Eti's headdress was a grand display, making her appear towering over her seated audience, who seemed small. The moonlight filtering through the thatching The moonlight filtering through the thatching accentuated its size creating a formidable presence around her. Draped in two pieces of cloth, one white and the other black, loosely tied at the shoulder, the hanging material added to her commanding presence. She exuded authority, and her audience see it. Even uncle Zano's father, usually a figure of authority himself, had to be meek and respectful during the proceedings. He understood well that any misstep on his part could result in being expelled and barred from future gatherings. He even had to guard his thoughts, ensuring they remained pure, as only such thoughts were deemed acceptable.

Pfumojena, speaking through Eti, stressed the significance of purity of mind, good character, sincere intentions, and love for humanity and nature. He made it clear that any deceitful behaviour, malevolent intentions, or involvement in black magic would not be tolerated. Such individuals would be exposed for who they truly were, and even their false humility would be their downfall. Pfumojena also cautioned against the deceit of false humility, emphasising the importance of genuine sincerity in all actions and intentions. Uncle Zano's father shuddered on hearing this pronouncement even though such admonitions were customary among spirit mediums.

For the first time in her life, Eti's lips touched beer. She took four gulps, emptying the gourd. It wasn't her choice to drink, but rather because Pfumojena used to take alcohol. Despite this, he wasn't known as a drunkard.

Eti rose to dance and at once, everyone joined in. Outside the singing and dancing continued. They sang *'ndabaiwa ndabaiwa kani, ndabaiwa nebanga jena (*I have been stabbed, I have been stabbed by a white machete)'* Pfumojena through Eti, stamped his feet in dance. With each stamp uncle Zano's father frowned. Finally, Pfumojena's spirit receded and the formalities ended. Eti left the room first, followed by the rest, streaming outside. Some headed straight for the beer, while others jumped onto the dance floor. It was a lively night. Amidst the merrymaking, Eti sat near the gate, her husband congratulating her. One by one, her brothers went to offer their congratulations, and I followed suit. After all, she was my mother. The event meant a lot to her, even though she had little choice but to accept it. It marked the launch of her career as Pfumojena's spirit medium. My daughters were there too. I wondered what Tarisai thought of the whole affair; it was her first such attendance. Whether she approved or not, I'd soon find out. Eti remained seated next to her husband, who was slowly getting drunk. That's the Eti we knew: a non-dancer and non-drinker.

There was sudden commotion as the crowd chanted, 'Mangondi, Ndingo, Ndingo' as most of his fans called him. He was nowhere to be found. Uncle Zano's father had dragged him behind the hut for questioning. He wanted an explanation as to why Eti was winning. Uncle Zano said, "You are a big body with no brains," as he shoved Mangondi away. Then, he rested his hands on his waist and stared at the night sky, shaking his head. Mangondi gathered himself dusting off his clothes. In the meantime, the sound of voices calling for the drummer was closing in on them.

"Voice down someone may hear us," Mangondi whispered.

"So, what! That won't change the fact that you are weak. A failure," Uncle Zano sneered.

Mangondi swallowed hard, his breath quickening audibly. Veins bulged in his hands, and his eardrums seemed to pulse. He narrowed his eyes and furrowed his brow. Before he could speak, a crowd shouted a short distance behind him. "There he is!"

Mangondi moved towards Uncle Zano's father, who retreated. With a confident stride, Mangondi whispered, "Now, that's a fact. You hear the crowd? I have a knack for drumming.

Excuse me, my fans are calling," Mangondi continued, leaving Uncle Zano's father standing still, aghast. Mangondi disappeared into the night with shouts of 'Ndingo, Ndingo' fading as they approached the yard. Just as well, Mangondi didn't disappoint. The unity of hand and hide mirrored the harmony of feet and ground, as even the dust ascended in a thick cloud.

Nancy enjoyed the drumming from a few huts away yet in full view of Mangondi thanks to the full moon. Her husband had left for the city on business.

"Oh Nancy, don't waste music away, let's go and dance," he urged. While tempted to look and answer, she ignored. Nancy tightened her grip on her shawl and kept her eyes fixed ahead, ignoring the voice behind her. But it seemed this persistent fool was determined to blow her cover. She recognised him from the first two words. He pronounced her name with a crescendo, making it easy for her to identify him by his voice.

Silence only seemed to fuel his persistence. "Ignore all you want, feisty brunette. I know it's you behind that shawl and brown make-up." Nancy bit her lip, resisting the urge to respond. Engaging him would only draw more attention to herself. "With looks like yours, it's hard not to take an interest," he continued, undeterred by her silence.

Nancy rolled her eyes while gritting her teeth as her disguise crumbled under his scrutiny.

"Apply it more often," he added.

With her disguise exposed, there was no point in staying silent. She retorted, "Who wouldn't notice you with that blob of glue on the front sole of your oversized Tenderfoot?" Their serious demeanour dissolved into laughter.

"And you know my feet feel lost in these shoes," then they chuckled more. They sat there instead of joining the dancing. Holding hands, they talked the night away giggling.

"How did you know it was me in that shawl?"

"Leave that, let's enjoy Mangondi's drumming huh."

* * *

The festivities of the night continued till after sunrise. Twice before the end, Eti went into the house and the spirit of Pfumojena came upon her. She instructed those of her family in attendance on certain important matters. She also gave guidance. Once or twice, she and her audience laughed on certain of her comments. Before sunrise she went into the hut again to close off the proceedings. Ululations, clapping and singing erupted in the hut and she exited first then others followed.

Outside, a few tough guys staggered about, challenging both the music and the beer. They boasted that they would be the last men standing, exchanging playful jibes. Murefu was one of the last to continue drinking. He'd only leave once he was sure there wasn't a drop of alcohol left in the pots. Either he'd doze off in the yard or some kind-hearted souls would transport him home in a wheelbarrow. No one would waste their cattle's energy by taking him home in a Scotch-cart.

Chapter 9

Tarisai reproached herself for attending the ceremony. Was it appropriate for someone of her calling to partake in such gatherings? Yet, this event was hosted by her own family. Could everyone else be mistaken? She cherished her grandmother dearly. In the past, she would seek guidance from her, but now, how could she approach her, especially on this matter? Would her grandmother be biased? Would she offer support while remaining objective, as she had done before? Tarisai tossed and turned on her mat. True, she hadn't been involved in any of the formalities. She refrained from participating in the activities, only indulging in the food, abstaining from beer, and refraining from singing or dancing. She remained an innocent bystander.

Zivai had come over for the event and she shared the room with Tarisai. "What's troubling the chatterbox so early in the morning. Even the elephants haven't gone to bath." Zivai chortled. Her laughter was an infectious one, at times would be misplaced, hence offending some of her listeners.

"You will never understand," Tarisai snapped turning away from her sister. Zivai though soft-spoken, level-headed, wasn't a pushover.

"Now you are wiser than me? Your philosophy is getting to your head."

"You see, exactly my point. You won't understand. Maybe if you stop being silly, I can share a thing or two with you."

Zivai grabbed a comb and shuffled to the door. She knew how to make her sister talk. Tarisai gave in to the bait and shouted.

"Was I wrong to attend grandmothers event? I'm confused. I can't tell right from wrong. The Apostle Paul's words in Romans, 'what we hate to do, that we do,' resonate with me. You know, the stories of Judas and Peter illustrate how people react differently to their mistakes. Judas felt guilty and condemned himself, while Peter sought redemption through self-reflection and change. This difference lies in the conviction and condemnation, which can be challenging to grasp at times, especially in moments like this. Right now, I just don't know what to think, because it involves family. Imagine if that were your husband? Well, how could I have married him without knowing material information? I don't know what's expected of me as a girl, a daughter, a granddaughter and as someone with a calling. Even as a girlfriend! Perhaps I'm destined for a life of celibacy and I should forget about marriage altogether—no dating. Err, no courtship," she remarked, her upper lip curled in a snarky expression. Her sister gave her a gentle push on her back while she laughed.

"What's that boy's name again? He's the headman's son, right?" Zivai winked while nudging her sister at the elbow with a mischievous grin.

Tarisai rolled her eyes and let out a deep sigh before continuing, "Before I'm called, I'm human. But I've also learnt that we are spiritual beings having a human experience. And, for grandma, she's Eti and she's Pfumojena. Both he and she in one. Masculine meets feminine, yet they harmonise without conflict. There are distinct differences."

"No that's not it. You see, there's so much you don't know. There's not always harmony"

"Just as your names suggests, you know everything Zivai. Get straight to the point."

Zivai fixated on cracking her peanuts and said, "You've become so religious lately." She furrowed her brows, frustration evident in her voice. "It feels like you're imposing your beliefs on everyone. It's as if you want us to sympathise with you." She let out an exasperated sigh, shaking her head. "We have our own problems. When I lost my husband, I felt overwhelmed when you mentioned how God gives and takes away. Why give in the first place? I'm a young widow raising a baby who may turn out to be a calamity if what Mbuya Zvirevo said stands." She glanced up briefly, her eyes narrowing. "Life doesn't revolve around you. Look around as your name says."

"What!" Tarisai's eyes widened, her tone defensive. "You know I am sorry about your late husband but we will all go, let not your heart be troubled. I'm just exploring my spirituality." She clasped her hands together, trying to maintain her composure. "It's important to me, and I'm not forcing anything on you or anyone else."

"Believe or not, it's changing you, and not in a good way." Zivai's voice softened slightly. "We used to be close, and now it feels like I don't even know you."

"I haven't changed who I am." Tarisai's shoulders slumped, her expression pained. "If anything, I'm trying to be a better person." She reached out, a pleading look in her eyes. "Why can't you respect that?"

"Respect goes both ways." Zivai's gaze softened, with a small smile painting on her face. "You act like you have all the answers, and it's frustrating, rather annoying."

"I'm not claiming to have all the answers." Tarisai's voice was gentle, tinged with sadness. "But my faith helps guide me." She took a deep breath, biting her lower lip. "Can't you accept that we might see things differently?"

"It just feels like you're distancing yourself from our family, from me." Zivai's voice wavered as her smile faded. She looked down, her eyes glistening with unshed tears. "It's hard to accept."

"Can't we find a middle ground where we respect each other's beliefs?" "I love our family," Tarisai affirmed, her tone filled with sincerity, "but I also need to be true to myself." Her eyes softened with empathy as she spoke, a gentle understanding woven into her words. "It's okay for you to honour our ancestors that way," she reassured. "I am not judging," she emphasised, her expression open and inviting. "But when I ask, I am also trying to know." A hint of curiosity flickered in her eyes. Zivai relaxed, meeting her sister's gaze with a glance of realisation. Tarisai continued, "We may not accept, but can't we find a middle ground where we respect each other's beliefs?" She spoke in an entreating tone, her words carrying a plea for reconciliation.

"Girls!" my husband, their father called. "Come to the kitchen, please." In the typical homestead setup, the kitchen served not only as a cooking area but also as a gathering place. Visitors were welcomed and hosted in kitchens. Built-in seats lined the walls, leaving designated spaces for other purposes. Traditionally, men occupied these footstools, while women and children sat on the floor. However, in our household, my husband allowed our daughters to sit on the footstools. His reasoning was simple: position shouldn't determine worth; intellect should!

We all exchanged pleasantries, and Tarisai wasted no time in heading straight to the pot on the fire, hoping to find porridge. Disappointed, she sank onto the footstool, while Zivai settled herself cross-legged on the floor.

"This goes especially for you, Tarisai," their father cautioned, his voice in a low tone. Be mindful of what you say to grandma or around her; we don't want to risk offending her. I know you can be quite the radical when it comes to these issues," he added, glancing briefly at Tarisai. He checked his watch, a habitual gesture of his when contemplating decisions.

"Now that you've finished secondary school," he continued, turning his attention back to Tarisai, "have you considered enrolling in an engineering apprenticeship? Our house in town is a walking distance from most of the factories, transport shouldn't be an issue."

Kindu was a mining town closest to our village, so we resided there in company houses. My husband worked as a conveyor belt operator. I didn't particularly mind where we stayed, but the town offered a more relaxing atmosphere, mainly due to the availability of electricity. With electricity, the burden of searching for firewood and chopping down trees was lifted. Additionally, pots remained unblackened by soot, and roofs stayed clear.

Our visits to the village were often prompted by Tarisai's persistent requests. When she was younger, she was convinced that she could uncover the link to the leopard's story by connecting with nature in the forest. Eager to keep her content, her father would give in to her wishes. During our trips to the village, Tarisai would scamper through the bushes, searching for inspiration and answers. This inclination of hers was one reason we eventually sent her away to boarding school - to redirect her focus and encourage socialisation.

"Tarisai, now that your sister has tasted married life, what do you want to do now that you've finished school?" father asked.

"Is that even a question to ask a child? She'll get married, of course," I added.

"Mother! No!" Tarisai said, clutching her temples. "I've been reading several articles, and I know what to do. Engineering is my path." She paused before adding, "Do you know Euler? He made me love math. What if my husband dies too?"

"Death is inevitable, that's beside the point here. You already have a boyfriend? Your mother never mentioned this Euler to me." Both sisters burst into laughter. Because Tarisai talked incessantly, Zivai became familiar with most of calculus, geometry, and trigonometry. She could recite Euler's identity and formula, Pythagoras, Descartes, Gauss, and her favourite 'character' was 'the walking polyglot' Maria Goretti.

"Father! Descartes is famous for saying 'I think, therefore I am,'" Zivai boasted, not to be outdone.

Tarisai immediately stopped her, "He copied from Apostle Paul who wrote 'I believe therefore I speak.'"

"Girls, get over yourselves, whose child is Euler?"

"Father, Leonhard Euler was a Swiss mathematician. We can discuss this another day. Of course, I will continue with my education. But before I do that, will you get baptised? Pretty please?"

I narrowed my eyes toward my husband, noticing that he nodded in response to Tarisai. However, his nod faltered into a half gesture as he froze blankly. He pulled his moustache. "We will discuss with your mother and get back to you, now go about your duties. We are done here."

Chapter 10

Euler is proof that a neurotic personality is not essential for mathematical prowess. He was just as ordinary as anyone else, unlike Einstein, whose genius often overshadowed his own humanity. Tarisai, however, felt a different calling, driven not by fame but by an inner fire to achieve greatness. Compelled by the Holy Spirit, she embarked on a journey to accomplish feats akin to a lion, despite her outward appearance as a lamb. Indeed, she was determined to excel and succeed, her resolve unwavering in the face of challenges. Her journey echoed the perseverance of Euler, whose ground-breaking work spanned the fields of calculus, geometry, and beyond. With each theorem and discovery, Tarisai found inspiration, driving her relentless pursuit of knowledge and excellence.

Moreover, Euler's contributions extended to astronomy, acoustics, music, and mechanics, sparking Tarisai's admiration for his diverse intellectual pursuits. Tarisai particularly found resonance with Euler's identity theorem, appreciating its elegance and significance. He made significant contributions to mathematics and engineering, showcasing the practical application of mathematical principles. It took months for me to understand the basics. Euler's identity ($e^{i\pi}$ + 1=0), named after the Swiss mathematician Leonhard Euler, who discovered it in the 18th century, is a revered equation uniting fundamental constants like π, i, and e. Mathematicians cherish Euler's identity for its simplicity and profound implications, reflecting the interconnectedness of mathematical concepts. Tarisai explained to me that Euler's identity is special because it combines five key constants—π, i, e, 0, and 1—with three basic mathematical operations: multiplication, exponentiation, and addition, each appearing exactly once. It looked so beautiful in Tarisai's notebooks. She stressed that this equation's simplicity is its beauty, as it reveals the intricate connections between these constants. Through Euler's identity, mathematicians can illustrate how the constants e, π, and i are related, showcasing the profound unity underlying mathematical concepts. Euler's identity is a celebrated equality in mathematics, often likened to a Shakespearean sonnet and hailed as 'the most beautiful equation. Once Tarisai drew that comparison to Shakespeare, everything clicked into place. I remembered listening to excerpts from Shakespeare during my time in Standard 6 at school, under the guidance of my beloved teacher, Mr. Winston

* * *

When Tarisai was fifteen years old, I recall her becoming entranced by a phrase that seemed to linger in her mind long after she first encountered it. The phrase was from a novel titled *"Ash Coal is the Colour of my True Love's Heart"*. Even now, in her thirties, the words echo in the recesses of her memory: *"The entire history of a love affair.* As she sat in the quiet of the lounge, the phrase resurfaced, as it often did. With a soft sigh, she spoke the words aloud, allowing them to hang in the air, heavy with significance, "The entire history of a love affair," she murmured, her voice barely above a whisper. "It's like... it's like the essence of life itself, distilled into a few simple words." In that moment, the words took on a new depth, resonating with a clarity that she hadn't fully appreciated before. They were more than just a passage from a book—they reflected her own journey, a reminder of the complexities of love, longing, and the human experience.

Recalling Tarisai's fascination with language and literature, I remembered another literary work that had left a lasting mark on her: Eugene Onegin. She had been captivated by the intricate tale of unrequited love and societal norms, drawing parallels between its themes and her own life experiences. Even now, in her thirties, she could still recall a paragraph she had committed to memory:

"The entire history of a love affair. The intensity of a man unaccustomed to strong emotions. Some believe that at fifteen, one's emotions are shallow. They overlook individuals like Juliet from Romeo and Juliet and Tatyana from Eugene Onegin. Age is not the sole determinant. Consider Eugene in Eugene Onegin; though he was young, he condescended to Tatyana, underestimated her, and treated her as a child. And, in the end, he came to realise his mistake when it was too late. So, I confessed my love to him directly, warning him to think carefully before losing something he might never have the chance to regain."

The memory of Tarisai's reflections on Eugene's treatment of Tatyana, coupled with her own words of warning to him, lingered in my mind. They were a testament to her depth of understanding and her willingness to confront life's complexities head-on. As her mother, I couldn't help but feel a sense of pride in Tarisai's steadfastness and resilience. Despite the challenges she faced in reconciling her aspirations with the realities of life, her unwavering dedication to her convictions filled me with admiration. Even amidst her struggles, Tarisai's unwavering commitment to pursuing her calling and embracing her intellect shone brightly, a testament to her remarkable spirit and unwavering determination.

While Zivai, her sister, had chosen a different path, one of settled married life, Tarisai's journey was marked by a different kind of bravery and determination. Whereas Zivai's contentment in her domestic life was admirable, Tarisai's pursuit of her calling and her unyielding quest for knowledge showcased a different kind of courage. Each sister, in her own way, exemplified strength and resilience, navigating life's complexities with grace and determination, albeit on divergent paths. I was just happy being there to witness my girls grow and glow. Regardless of the paths they chose, my pride in them remained unwavering. As I savoured my beer, I reflected on the journey that had led me to this moment. Despite the challenges I faced and the unconventional choices I made, even my own mother, Eti, found pride in me. Despite the hardships I put her through by refusing to conform to tradition and marry, her pride in my unwavering spirit never faltered. The sudden sound of music startled me, prompting me to step outside. There, I found Mangondi.

Chapter 11

A Walkman radio slung over his shoulder, Mangondi always played "Pemberai" and "Gwindingwi," by Thomas Mapfumo, much to the annoyance of everyone, including the dogs. Whenever he approached with his Walkman blaring, the village dogs would start barking. He claimed that his distant friend and musician, Thomas Mapfumo, had given him the portable radio and cassettes so he could listen to his songs on the go. However, the village leaders, including my father and an elder with hair as white as a cotton field, had different opinions. They asserted that all other radio programs and songs were rubbish, and the only exciting and informative station was the one broadcasting from Lourenço Marques in Mozambique. They liked the songs by Thomas Mapfumo and anything from Lourenço Marques in Mozambique. I always enjoyed listening to them defend and praise that station. Sometimes, I even poked them intentionally to fuel the discussion further.

Lourenço Marques in Mozambique was more than just a radio station; it was a beacon of truth in a sea of propaganda. Unlike the national radio stations, which often served as mouthpieces for the government, Lourenço Marques provided unbiased news reporting and a platform for diverse voices to be heard. Its commitment to journalistic integrity made it a trusted source of information, especially during times of political unrest and censorship. In addition to its news programming, Lourenço Marques also offered a wide range of music, showcasing artists from across Africa and beyond. Its eclectic playlists featured everything from traditional folk songs to the latest hits, making it a favourite among listeners seeking an alternative to the mainstream fare offered by state-controlled stations. For those of us living in Rhodesia, tuning in to Lourenço Marques was more than just a form of entertainment; it was a lifeline to the outside world. Whether it was hearing about the latest developments in neighbouring countries or progression of the liberation struggles, or simply enjoying the music, listening to Lourenço Marques offered a glimpse of a reality beyond the confines of government propaganda. I recall one local news anchor who was arrested by the regime after saying, "*Hedzinoi nhema dzichiverengwa naPami* (Here are the lies read by Pami)." That was towards the end of the war, so fortunately, he did not serve a long jail sentence.

The other topical issue which went wild was that fungi beverage which we drank and it apparently nourished us. It seemed to have emerged from the Far East, although it was rumoured that the few Chinese present in the country never consumed this fungi. The frenzy over this peculiar fungi swept through the township like wildfire. It was astonishing to witness the entire town captivated by this newfound obsession. Caught up in the excitement, I, too, neglected to approach the situation with a critical eye. Where did this fungi originate? China, they said. But were the Chinese consuming it as well? I couldn't help but entertain wild theories, like it being a deliberate attempt to eradicate certain populations, perhaps even targeted at us in the high-density suburbs.

The method of consumption was simple enough. A small portion could be divided among multiple households, spreading its influence far and wide. All it required was a pot of cold tea poured into the container with the fungi. As the fungi absorbed the tea, it swelled up, ready to be broken into chunks and shared among other households. Those given would in turn give others once it swelled up after fermentation. The juice extracted from the fungi became a popular nutritious and filling beverage, sweetened with sugar like any other tea. We could spend the whole day feasting on this fungi beverage then wait for supper. Supposedly, there were numerous health benefits associated with it, though I remained sceptical.

Despite the widespread consumption, I noticed no changes in myself. I maintained my regular fitness routine at the local sports ground, and the daily chores of washing and ironing kept me active. It became increasingly evident that food regulations in the country were lax, allowing for such crazes to take hold without scrutiny.

* * *

I'd sent Tarisai to boarding school in order to wean her off her father who gave her too much freedom and normalised her weird life. Somehow, I began to understand. She was under an illusion and I intended to help her out. She changed schools within six months of starting. Just after two terms. Similar to her grandmother, she had amassed some enemies within her class and those of other senior stream liked her.

"She thinks she's too intelligent to hang out with us. We'll surely teach her a lesson," said a gang leader in Tarisai's class.

"With this letter, she's done for," she concluded and her followers guffawed as she crushed the piece of paper in her hands. They had penned a love letter in reply to the torn one they had found in the classroom bin. They didn't know the writer of the first letter, but as for the second one, they planned to make everyone believe that it was from Tarisai. The student who thought she was special.

The second school rule stated dating and all its connotations were prohibited on school premises. That letter if reported was a guarantee of trouble with the authorities. Just as well, the math teacher stumbled upon the planted half torn reply and read it aloud.

"I know we are meant for each other. My dimple on the right and yours on the left makes us a perfect match. We are a lovely music sheet and I will play us the harmonica every note of our love. See you behind the dining hall same time. Tarisai."

The teacher looked at her meaningfully and gestured with her finger to follow her immediately. Both student and teacher were equally shocked. That was so unlike Tarisai, there had to be a mistake. Most of her classmates hit their desks and danced in victory.

Tarisai was suspended. The headmaster announced Tarisai's suspension and she slipped into a chair. It didn't take long before she recollected herself and stood up.

"I'm speaking the truth. You know I lead Scripture Union and Christian Students Fellowship. That wasn't me. I'm being framed."

"We hear you, until proved otherwise, you are suspended. Maybe you have other evidence."

Tarisai feeling defeated, shuffled out headed to the hostels. She had until the next day to vacate the school. She had cried on other days but not today. She cleaned her ukulele ready to play it to comfort herself.

"King David played the harp. I will be fine. What is wrong with me though?"

"In the Bible, Jesus Himself said 'to whom much is given, much is expected. And a prophet isn't accepted in his own hometown."

"Is this my destiny? Is this the price for having this calling? This great responsibility. The Holy Spirit is the Wonderful Counsellor, Comforter and Advocate."

"What just happened back in there? How can I comfort others when I don't have comfort?

"I know some of my classmates dislike me, but to this extent? This short space of time and this. Just because I command a huge following."

She knew that I'd be furious with her suspension news so she intended to inform her father first. He was her safe place. That night on her rusty singe bed, she tossed and turned a thousand times looking at her glow watch every time.

"But no, I won't cry. Not this time, not ever again," she comforted herself sniffing for the last time and dozed off.

Chapter 12

As the headman's son, Tikana, left the village for the bustling mining town of Kindu, he found himself in the company of his childhood friend, Tarisai, who had also moved to urban life seeking new opportunities. The nostalgic familiarity of their shared past soon blossomed into a deeper connection, and their hearts found comfort in each other's presence.

However, as fate would have it, another friend from the village, Henry, entered the scene. Henry, charismatic and charming, became a close companion to Tikana. One evening, under the town's stars, Henry confessed his love to Tarisai, creating a ripple of tension in their trio. Tarisai, torn between loyalty to Tikana and the unexpected attraction she felt for Henry, found herself entangled in a complex emotional web.

Tikana, sensing the shifting dynamics, confronted Tarisai, "Is there something unsaid between us, dear? "

Tarisai hesitated, struggling to find the words, "Tikana, our friendship means the world to me, but there's something I need to tell you. "

Before she could reveal her feelings, Henry intervened, expressing his love for Tarisai. Tikana, blindsided by the revelation, felt a profound sense of betrayal from both his friend and the woman he thought he could trust. The town, once a canvas for their shared dreams, now witnessed the fracture of their relationships. Tikana, grappling with heartache, distanced himself from the duo, leaving Tarisai torn between the friend she had known since childhood and the unexpected allure of Henry.

The love triangle played out against the backdrop of the town's relentless pace, leaving the trio to navigate the complexities of friendship, loyalty, and unspoken desires. In the end, the township became a canvas not only for dreams but also for the bittersweet brushstrokes of love and heartbreak.

Tikana, despite the initial hurt, chose to prioritise the long-standing bond he shared with Tarisai. In a heartfelt conversation, he acknowledged the depth of their connection and the importance of their enduring friendship. Tikana's maturity in handling the situation surprised Tarisai, leading her to reassess her feelings.

Henry, realising the impact of his actions on both Tikana and Tarisai, showed remorse and took responsibility for the unintended consequences of his confession. The trio decided to redefine their relationships, opting for a path of understanding and forgiveness. As time unfolded, the bonds of friendship between Tikana, Tarisai, and Henry evolved. They navigated the complexities of love and friendship, learning valuable lessons about communication, trust, and the resilience of genuine connections. After three weeks, Tikana expressed his love for Tarisai and she confessed she felt same way for him. Henry was happy for them and he told them he had found apprenticeship in a border town and would be leaving at the end of the month.

One day as they were having lunch at Machipisa Café, the trio shared some light-hearted memories until suddenly Tikana sighed, shaking his head in frustration.

"Tarisai, I am getting a little tired. I thought it was a phase. But It's not just a phase; you are pushing her beliefs onto everyone, acting like you have got it all figured out. "

Henry shrugged dismissively, "Maybe she's just evolving, unlike some people stuck in their narrow-minded views. "

Tarisai was still open-mouthed at the sudden outburst. She gently but firmly interjected, "This isn't about narrow-mindedness. I'm just trying to find meaning in my life."

Tikana waved his hand, "Meaning? Please. It's probably some trendy spiritual awakening. I will not let you drag me into your delusional world."

Henry then stepped forward, his tone firm. "Everyone has the right to explore their beliefs without judgment. I support you Tarisai. You are independent and not yet married to him anyway."

Tikana rolled his eyes again, scoffing and said, "Oh, spare me the preachy nonsense. I bet you're just as brainwashed as she is. Your father benefited a lot from the missionaries when he was a headmaster."

Tarisai spoke up, her voice tinged with frustration. "Leave his father out of it. "This is my personal journey. Can't you respect that?"

Tikana snaped back, "Your 'journey is driving a wedge between not just us, but your family too. Hope it's worth it." He exhaled heavily, looking torn, "I can't believe you're letting your wayward beliefs ruin everything. It's like you're replacing our connection with this religious nonsense."

Tarisai held back tears, her expression pained, "I'm not replacing anything. I just want you to understand what's important to me. Maybe I am meant to be celibate after all, these are just signs."

Tikana shook his head, his frustration evident. "Important? It's becoming an obsession. I didn't sign up for a relationship with a zealot."

Tarisai lost it and lashed out, "Hey, ease up. I'm just trying to figure things out."

Tikana ran a hand through his hair, looking defeated, "Figure things out? You're turning into someone I don't recognise, and I'm not sure I like it."

Tarisai had tears well up in her eyes, visibly looking torn between her beliefs and her relationship. "I thought you'd support me through this journey."

Tikana squeezed her hand and paused, his expression conflicted, "I can't support you losing yourself in some dogma. Maybe you need to choose between this faith and our relationship. I am not pressuring you. I just need more time with you."

* * *

As Tikana and Tarisai's love blossomed, such complexities arose and became frequent. Tikana furrowed his brow, concern evident in his eyes, "I've noticed the tension between us two, and it's concerning. It seems like the differences in religious beliefs are causing a rift."

Tarisai took a deep breath and sunk her shoulders. "It's not just about the beliefs. I have not changed, and you may feel like I am choosing her faith over our relationship and spending more time at Scripture Union, but I still make time for you. It's not like we always see each other daily, sweetheart."

Tikana nodded slowly, rubbing his chin, "I understand it can be challenging to balance time but I know this something meaningful to you. All I am asking is when I am around can you cancel attending Scripture Union. You can always go another day."

Tarisai almost choked on her saliva and grabbed her mouth. Her hand fidgeting nervously. "I don't want anything to come between us. However, my faith is personal, and it shouldn't affect our bond. You cannot make me choose Tiki."

Tikana then reached out to gently squeeze her hand. He explained that it was not about her faith coming between them. He also added, "It's about feeling like I've lost my sweetie to something I don't fully understand."

Tarisai offered a small smile, trying to reassure him, "Change is inevitable, and people grow in different ways. Maybe finding common ground or learning more about my beliefs could help bridge the gap." Tikana then leaned in and whispered, something that made her giggle.

Tarisai explained that communication was key and that they should all try to listen and respect each other's perspectives. The couple's frequent arguments about faith and their relationship persisted, reflecting immaturity but also echoing issues faced by couples of all ages. My priority was for them to concentrate on their engineering vocational school studies. I wasn't confident about where this relationship was heading. Perhaps Tarisai would be better off embracing her faith and following in the footsteps of Apostle Paul, as she had insisted for years. I relied on Olivia, Tarisai's level-headed friend for her sense of practicality and sensibility. She was my secret weapon, even though she wasn't aware of it.

One time, we had invited Mbuya Zvirevo for a breather at our house in Kindu. Coincidentally, Olivia and that headman's son showed up to offer their regards. As anticipated, the conversation inevitably veered into a discussion about faith, dancing delicately with tradition on its tiptoes. Tarisai always found a way to bring this topic up.

Tarisai furrowed her brows. "I feel a calling to serve a greater purpose through my Christian faith."

Mbuya Zvirevo shook her head and said, "Your so-called calling is leading you away from our traditions. This Christianity of yours is not what our family has followed for generations. When did Vasco da Gama arrive here?"

Tarisai nodded, "I respect our family's traditions, granny, but my faith is important to me. I believe I can still honour our roots while following my calling."

Mbuya Zvirevo then folded her arms and said, "Your calling has no place in our ceremonies. It's pulling you away from our ancestors."

Tarisai clasped her hands and cleared her throat. "I want to find a way to bridge the gap, to show that my beliefs can coexist with our family's traditions. The Bible says we should obey our parents."

Olivia who had been reading a newspaper rolled her eyes and said, "Your family drama is getting old. You're torn between your Christian calling and this ancient family tradition. Pick a side already."

Tarisai raised her voice slightly. "I'm trying to find a middle ground, a way to respect both."

To this Olivia chuckled crossing her arms. "Middle ground? You're just weakening your beliefs to please everyone. Stand firm in your convictions."

Tarisai's annoying boyfriend interjected gently, "Maybe there's a way for both to coexist without compromising her faith."

Olivia scoffed and frowned. "Coexist? This isn't some utopia. Life is about choices. What's more important, your faith or this family drama?"

Mbuya Zvirevo knew when to let sleeping dogs lie. She went to the verandah to bask in the twilight, leaving Tarisai to grapple with her emotions. "It's not that simple, " Tarisai murmured between sobs. "I love my family, and I love my faith."

Olivia leaned forward, her voice a hiss, "Well, it looks like you're heading for a collision. Either your family accepts your calling or you risk losing them. Maybe it is time to be alone with no boyfriend influencing your decisions too." She had nailed it, I smirked. That boy had to leave the equation.

As tensions rose, Olivia pushed Tarisai to confront the difficult choice between her Christian calling and the expectations of their family's traditional beliefs. Tarisai stormed from the room, slamming the door. Olivia then shouted after her, "Running away won't solve anything! You're just avoiding the inevitable."

That week, Tarisai sought refuge with her uncle, Mike. She yearned to understand what the Bible teaches about free will. Uncle Mike patiently explained that the Bible acknowledges the concept of free will, emphasising that individuals have the freedom to make choices and face the consequences. Tarisai poured out her conflicted feelings, torn between her Christian calling and the expectations of her family's traditions. Uncle Mike offered guidance, suggesting that the Bible encourages believers to seek wisdom and understanding. Perhaps her calling and the family's traditions weren't mutually exclusive; finding a balance was key. He understood her concern that her beliefs might be seen as a threat to their traditions.

As they parted, Uncle Mike's words lingered, "Remember, understanding takes time. Share your thoughts with empathy and be open to listening. The Bible teaches us to love and respect one another."

Uncle Mike should have been made a leader at Tarisai's church, especially after I heard how they treated her at one time. Upon returning to her church that weekend from her uncle, my daughter faced ostracism due to her open-mindedness towards her family's traditions, especially her grandmother's role as a spirit medium.

Some elders said to her, "You're associating with spirit mediums now? Have you lost your way? We hear you attend their ceremonies."

She answered in a murmur, lacking confidence in her response. "I haven't lost my way. I'm trying to bridge the gap between my faith and our family's traditions. It doesn't mean I've abandoned Christianity."

The elder snapped at her. "Well, it's not something we can accept. You're making us uncomfortable."

With the weight of judgment apparent, my daughter grappled with the challenge of being shunned by some in her Christian community for embracing the diversity within her family. The struggle to find acceptance and understanding continued. I believe they could have handled the matter in a more amicable way. Tolerance. Gentility. Love. I know her pastor and his wife occasionally reached out to her to strengthen her and encourage her. While Tarisai grappled with the judgment of her Christian community, my own thoughts drifted to the contrasting symbolism of lions. In the Bible, the Lion of Judah represents Jesus Christ, embodying strength, courage, and leadership, a powerful force for righteousness. Conversely, in our tradition and culture, the lion 'Mhondoro' is revered as not only the king of the jungle, but as an object of ancestral worship, symbolising, wisdom, protection and also the presence of ancestral spirits, serving as guardians of the land and guiding us. Despite the differences in cultural interpretation, both lions reflect the resilience and guidance sought in navigating the complexities of faith and heritage. As I pondered these symbolic representations, I saw the common attributes of reverence, strength and protection. However, I didn't understand why Tarisai's Bible called Jesus the lion and the lamb. Well, I needed a distraction from these deep and confusing thoughts, so I watched football on TV.

Growing up we knew of Pele, the king of football. Tarisai and her cronies called him the 'GOAT' (Greatest of All Time) . Even the newspapers and TV showered praises on him. In my days calling someone a goat was an insult leading to a possible fight. Goats are known as stubborn, playful, silly and annoying especially compared to other livestock. I sipped on some beer while watching a soccer match.

Chapter 13

Daughter, Tarisai again

It all started when Tarisai was watching a wildlife documentary on television. We were one of the few households with TVs in Kindu those days soon after independence. People would flock to watch wrestling and soccer on our black and white four-legged TV. On quiet weekdays, I allowed Tarisai to watch cartoons, wildlife documentaries, and shows like Skippy. She also enjoyed local dramas like Paraffin and Mukadota. Nevertheless, it bothered me that she refused to play with most of her agemates and preferred to stay indoors. My husband saw nothing wrong with that and labelled me paranoid. Her older sister, Zivai, was the outgoing, free-spirited one. She mostly cared about traditional ceremonies, superstitions, her looks, and feminine appeal. I knew she would marry quite early, and I was right.

Tarisai sat there watching the late afternoon animal show while I ironed her father's work suits. A baby leopard was trapped on a sharp-edged tree stump, its hide pierced in a way that it couldn't free itself. In fact, the sharp edge cut through the cub. All the cub could do was wince as it tried to free itself. The more it moved, the more it whimpered. The mother stopped her attempts to pull her cub upon realizing she was hurting it more. The mother sobbed in helplessness. Tarisai wept as if in agony like the cub. I dashed to switch off the TV as the scene became too graphic, noticing the trauma in her conduct. I could not allow her to see those disturbing scenes; it was wrong.

"Well, ethics on wildlife documentaries state that photographers should not interfere in the ecosystem. Those men were not on a rescue mission." That is what I had always told her and she had the same reply almost all the time.

"That could have been avoided; the helpless cub could have been saved. What did the crew do? I want to know what happened to her, mum," Tarisai exclaimed, her concern evident in her voice.

"Alright, princess, tell me, how do you know the cub was female?" I asked, intrigued.

"It was quite obvious, those almond eyes and the pretty smile like Snow White. All fit for a girl," she asserted.

She had maintained the same nature of questions. I tried to divert her attention but all my efforts were futile. Her obsession with that animal was disturbing. It was worrying me each day and her father wasn't much help in dissuading her.

"Give her time, she's still growing, she will eventually grow out of it."

My mother was right, that the absence of my husband's support in some of these seemingly trivial issues would make it difficult for me to manage Tarisai. I could see her wayward nature developing. But there wasn't much we could do as her parents since she claimed she was called by the Holy Spirit. She had a divine call upon her life and she intended to fulfill her purpose. After she saw that documentary, she became extremely inquisitive.

Finally, I thought I had convinced that the trapped cub was rescued by some scouts and took her to a vet in the vicinity. I comforted her, telling her that help can arrive. The baby leopard, despite its suffering, was eventually healed and cared for at a conservatory. It showed the dedication of those who protect wildlife. It was such a relief that she bought the story. The image of a cub trapped like that was traumatic especially for a child her age, which is why we had to erase those images from her. Grown as I was, I shuddered at the mere visualisation of the cub's predicament, what more my little girl. She was indeed tormented. I do not understand why this gory film had no parental advisory tab. We do not know how the documentary ended and I was not too concerned at that time.

I do not know which of the two was better, being asked about the leopard or being told that her mission was to save others and that the cub was a sign. When she turned eighteen, her focus shifted towards fulfilling her mission, with reference to the cub once again. Then, in May of that year, we went to Njanja, and the magic happened. Maybe the God Tarisai believed in had answered my prayer about her fussing over the cub. It was an unhealthy obsession that she fixated on that cub, even after years of seemingly forgetting about it.

"Mum, you know that it is written in the Holy Bible that in the beginning was the Word, and the Word was with God and the Word was God. You know that right?"

"What are you going on about, should I take down notes ma'am?" I chided.

"Even Jesus wasn't accepted in his hometown, you know," Tarisai mumbled at my sarcasm.

I was a Christian alright only by virtue of attending scripture union class at the dressmaking school which was free. Classes were free otherwise, I would not have enrolled. The local teacher gave all students a little blue book which was palm size. This book was the New Testament of the Bible and the teacher would narrate stories from the Old Testament and link them to the New Testament which we had. Honestly, I was only there for the free tailoring classes. Yes, some of the stories from the book were intriguing and out of this world, but I just wondered if indeed any of them truly happened. I remember the story of one Gideon who was asked to go to battle with three thousand men, and then he was asked to make them drink water, and those who lapped like dogs were selected. What an odd selection! Commanders apply strategy in battle not that.

Of the remaining soldiers, he was asked to let them sleep, and those who fell asleep flat were kicked out. Again, that was unrealistic. He went on to win the battle with three hundred men against an army of thirty thousand. And that little boy who slew the giant Goliath with a sling and stone, even Mangondi, though smaller than Goliath, would not have fallen in that manner. There were so many stranger-than-fiction tales and some fairly realistic ones, and Tarisai strongly believed them all. I remained sceptical, although inwardly, I felt drawn to Tarisai's faith. An even crazier one was when water was turned into wine. Wow. Tarisai believed otherwise. She was so immersed in her faith that she claimed she was chosen to save others, to spread news of the person of the Holy Spirit. My mother, Eti, who was now commonly known as Mbuya Zvirevo, was the extreme opposite of Tarisai, yet they had similarities. It seemed I was the neutral one. I was neither here nor there. I knew there was a higher power ordering events in the universe through humans and nature, and I had no special role in that; I was simply part of the audience. Whenever, Tarisai met with her grandmother, there was some degree of natural tension, so to say. Neither party was hostile to the other, but there was an uncanny atmosphere in their presence, yet they loved each other so much.

Tarisai continued, "All I am saying, mum, is that as part of my assignment, I should go to Njanja and meet granny's other family. Isn't that where her other brother is, the one who worked as a security officer during the Chimurenga war?" That was her new song, daily we would work up to its lyrics.

One night she crept to her father who was perusing the past week's newspapers for sports news. "Dad, these days I am meditating John chapter 1." He knew her well enough to anticipate where this story was leading and what she wanted. More importantly, my husband was a converted Christian, and he had a deep understanding of the Bible. He attended lessons with some clergymen at the community hall. His name was changed from Tazivei to John upon baptism, but most of the folk maintained his old name. So, Tarisai knew that he would always have her vote of confidence. They clicked in that regard, which is also why he never coerced her into thinking about marriage even at a later stage. He knew she intended to follow Apostle Paul's path of celibacy. She felt called, and he gave her all the support he could. After a short session of father and daughter talk, she rose to leave for bed, smiling.

"My lovely wife, here's some money, this week make plans with Tarisai to visit Njanja. There's also enough to buy groceries and carry with you. Let me know when you decide on the date."

My husband had changed a lot from the time of his conversion into Christianity. He became friends with the clerics, and slowly, I felt I was losing him. There was a total paradigm shift, his conduct and his line of reasoning. Even his dressing, he started wearing safari shorts, denim trousers and t-shirts. Yet, all the while he used to wear polycotton trousers and viscose shirts. I noticed a meekness in his disposition; although he was largely phlegmatic, he became more sanguine. Even the way he handled matters in our home, he wasn't manly anymore. He was no longer that imposing husband my father married me off to on that fateful day of the baby baboon event. Even my father would have shed tears of impunity. Of his masculinity, only his biological makeup remained. Anyway, it was good to get away from him a bit, so I looked forward to going to Njanja.

Chapter 14

An aromatic stench filled our nostrils in welcome. What greeted us was quite a phenomenal sight of decomposing meat and a trail of green and black flies left in a quiet single file as if to make space for the visitors in the small kitchen. Meat hung like a pile of blankets on the overhead smoke-covered wooden beams. It was haphazardly thrown but all this was deliberate. When the procession of flies left, a fat creamish wriggly movement covered the beef in white. Tripe, intestines, spleen, liver, brisket, oxtail and all sorts of pieces were heaped. After what seemed an eternity stuck at the door in astonishment, we shambled into the warm hut.

Initially, the smell was appalling but eventually our faces lit up in the hut embracing the inevitable aroma.

"That's *mvumvira*, really tasty," an old woman volunteered upon noticing that our eyes remained engrossed in awe. Let me roast some for you." Immediately, I clutched my tummy nauseated already. Then she grabbed a chunk and shook it, with some worms falling into the fire.

"Don't worry, the heat will kill them, " she explained, gesturing towards a good batch of fat maggots clinging tightly to the meat. Their home was the decomposing, semi-preserved meat. It was the only home they knew.

"Alternatively, we heap it up for a few days and dump it into those two pots over there, and impressively it matures into this aromatic flavourful meat. It's a delicacy in these parts of the Save."

"How can you brag without mentioning me?" another shaky voice giggled. "I am your grandma's brother, the third boy in the family." He walked over to turn some cinders back onto the beef. "You know, during the height of the armed struggle, I was detained for activism at Hohoho restriction camp, along with others. As prisoners, we each had duties in and around the buildings, farm work, domestic work you name it." We all listened intently, our eyes fixed on him, captivated by his words and the weight of his experiences. "Your uncle, this one here who shaved a white man bald, was a guard. So, of all duties, I was exempt from that of emptying the toilet," he chuckled, reminiscing about the past with a mix of pride and humour.

Tarisai interjected, "Toilet, huh?"

He sneered again before continuing. "All excretions were collected in a common bucket placed at the back of the room. We urinated outside in random places. With six of us sharing the cell, one of us would have to carry the twenty-litre bucket to the Blair toilet outside once a week. Whether it was full, overflowing, or not, it had to be emptied. The safest method was to balance it on the head, slanting the head backwards. Any spilling would fall straight behind. Holding the bucket by the hand meant feet would be drenched in faeces, not to mention the risk of splashing on clothes and faces. That was a grim reality of our circumstances."

Tarisai opened her mouth, aghast and frowning as if she could picture the poop-carrying men. "That's roughly 3.5 litres of human waste per person over six days. Phenomenal," she remarked, her tone a mix of disbelief and grim fascination.

"So, your uncle here saved me from doing that disgusting duty." The whole room resounded with laughter.

"Now let's all settle down and enjoy some warm food, wont' we?" grandma said, smiling warmly, her words offering a comforting contrast to the hilarious, yucky, disturbing tales shared moments before.

What an amusing welcome. I had taken Tarisai and her cousins to Njanja to meet her grandmother's brother. He had relocated with his family and settled on the banks of the mighty Save River. Tarisai's constant nagging had finally persuaded me to travel all this way. She was ever asking about her family. For a long time, she had listened to charming stories, and she had an inkling that Njanja had a link to the little leopard.

Over the coming days, we continued to gather around the fire after supper or lounged under the shade of the mango trees mid-afternoon, enjoying each other's company and sharing stories. For evening meals, Tarisai took on the responsibility of washing dishes outside in the morning, rising early to complete the task.

In the corner of the yard, sat an old Morris next to the well. Uncle Mhasvi had received this obsolete piece of junk, which they called a car, as a gift for his service as a loyal guard. Despite its outdated appearance, it was his prized possession. He would polish it once a week, and Tarisai sought to understand the attachment he felt toward such a vehicle.

"Now you are here and asking about it, that's the whole point. It triggers imagination, creativity and ingenuity. It's not just a car. It's a piece of inspiration."

"Very well then uncle." The two discussed in detail as Tarisai asked countless questions. Despite being a chatterbox, she could listen for hours on end. It is from this conversation that she said realisation struck her. All these years it wasn't about the leopard per se; it was about how she could impact her environment for change. With her strong will, how she could influence others for change. Influencing systems and structures for the advancement of society. Hers was the spiritual front, the psychological aspect of those around her. She realised she would encounter setbacks and all sorts of hindrances, but resilience would propel her on this mission. She finally understood, and henceforth, she laid the leopard story to rest and focused on the future. It was our fourth day in Njanja, and I was happy to see that the trip was paying off.

"What's that continuous sound?" Tarisai asked Uncle Mhasvi.

"Those are hippos, far away in the Save River, they bath, play and live there."

"Do you eat them?"

Chuckling, "We don't see eye to eye, no we don't eat them. Come on let's go inside."

It was amazing how fast we had grown accustomed to the *mvumvira* aroma. It was delightfully addictive and surprisingly yummy. Two of my mother's brothers had settled here purely because they were adventurous, and I am glad they had. This trip solved my number one problem of the leopard. This place worked magic.

The following days were uneventful. Tarisai pestered her grandma to teach her to play *chipendani* (plucked string instrument).

"How about I teach you to play a leaf instead?"

"A leaf?" Tarisai said almost choking with suppressed laughter.

"A leaf Tari. Children of nowadays." She said smiling while shaking her head. Tarisai enjoyed singing but she sang out of tune, the discord was unbearable she resorted to playing instruments instead. She liked wind instruments and she was slowly mastering the flute. A string instrument like *chipendani* would be an interesting addition. Learning to play a leaf was also a good and inexpensive idea.

The night before our planned departure, Tarisai inquired about the great Uncle Mhasvi's feat that led him to be a security guard after committing an alleged crime.

"This bubbly man to your right, Tarisai's mum, is great Uncle Mhasvi who is renowned for being the first black man to illegally shave a white man's head. He sneaked behind him, grabbed him by the collar simultaneously sitting on his torso and running a two scissors over his head." We all laughed thus interrupting grandma from continuing. "Believe it or not, let me finish," she gathered some phlegm and spat into the fire.

"The poor white man fidgeted and wrestled, but to no avail. As you can still see, your uncle's now droopy muscles were once stringy and bulky. He was sinewy. He left the man bald. By the time he finished with the haircut, a sizable crowd surrounded them, with a lot of guffawing overshadowing muffled chuckles. Some feared arrest for laughing at the superior white, while others laughed openly with so much excitement that they sang.

He was arrested for undermining the white man's superiority, assault and treason. These charges were so serious that he was sentenced to death."

"How absurd, just for that!" Tarisai blurted astonished.

It was somewhat hard for those born post-war to fully comprehend the gravity of the liberation struggle.

"So, on the day of his execution, he intricately carved an escape plan. With help from fellow inmates, he dug a hole by the jail fence and opened it to let the prisoners escape. When only a few prisoners remained, he then raised an alarm that there was a prison break and he pretended to be wrestling one man to stop him from living. The guards were puzzled that someone on death sentence remained waiting for his supposed demise. He was then freed on account of honesty given the circumstances and was consequently awarded a merit role as a constabulary. Yes, that's him, your clever great uncle. They also made him a security officer, where he left with that cherished Morris in the yard." Laughter filled the kitchen, and I never got tired of hearing this account. What a lovely finish to our journey. In many ways, this trip yielded much more than I'd expected. Tarisai was returning home a better person. She even accepted to carry some *mvumvira* home.

Chapter 15

Tarisai turned out a rounded person after her stint at boarding school despite the petty boarders' squabbles. Even her trip to Njanja yielded much for hr overall outlook in social life. She was so excited to show off her leaf playing skills, gathered some of her peers. She also thought by interacting with them, they could get to understand her.

"Someone please get me a leaf from that tree by the gate." Tarisai said. There was commotion as two girls raced to the tree. She folded it ready to play. The sound was marred.

"This is somewhat sticky, it's supposed to be silky. Please get me a clean leaf." She ran her fingers over it and it felt slippery and butting her lips, a bitter taste met her. "Weird," she murmured.

She wiped her lips with her hand unaware she was spreading the sticky stuff. She played the new leaf for about thirty seconds before she started feeling her lips bulging. The sound became inaudible again. Throwing the leaf on impulse, she ran inside straight to the mirror. She called herself the girl who never screams but for the first time she did. I ran into the bathroom only to find her frozen. Her lips were swollen, chin had blisters and eyes were bloodshot. I hadn't seen her so frightened. I knew basic first aid taught at the dressmaking school. I also knew natural remedies as taught by my elders at the village. I immediately remembered the nurses I frowned upon who paced the corridors of Harare Hospital. Well, some of them scowled, strutted and ignored patients. They brought the nursing fraternity to disrepute, nevertheless, I was grateful for the opportunity to learn treatment of basic injuries, cuts and abrasions sponsored by volunteer nurses from Harare Hospital. They attended our dressmaking classes to teach us first aid and CPR. My mind raced back to reality in as second.

"Did you drink that thinners over there by mistake, or that pesticide, did you?" I kept calm avoiding any sign of panic.

"No!" she yelled covering both ears. I gave her a reassuring look, handing her a cup of water to gargle.

"I don't know. I-I-wait, that sticky leaf," she said rushing outside leaving me tagging behind. Her audience had packed themselves into the house, all looking concerned. Both leaves lay where she dropped them.

"I played these mother and this one felt sticky and tasted funny I replaced it with that one."

I examined both leaves and sniffing, I quickly figured what went wrong. "Did you pick them yourself?"

"No, this gluey one came from Laina and the clean one from Olivia. What is it?"

I explained to her that Laina had intentionally laced the leaf with the milky extract of that shrub near the gate and that caused an allergic reaction which could have turned deadly. All the girls now gathered at the verandah were shocked as I narrated. I rubbed aloe vera gel around her chin to reduce inflammation. Eti my mother had insisted that I plant the aloe shrub as a necessity. I dragged Tarisai with one hand to face the girls.

"Are you happy now? This is what you wanted right?" I said eyes narrowed towards Laina.

"Leave Laina. You are worse than a criminal."

The crowd exchanged bewildered looks, muttering amongst themselves. "We just saw her run—"

"Quiet!" I cut the speaker off.

Laina shuffled from the back head bowed down as the crowd booed. "How could you, what have I done to you?" Tarisai asked teethed clenched. Laina continued the long walk of shame in silence and once out of sight, they consoled Tarisai whose eyes were already clearing. The girls shared about how generally mean Laina was and how she constantly spoke against Tarisai. Her sister Olivia looking embarrassed, apologised heartily. Olivia was genuinely fond of Tarisai and the feeling was mutual. This is how their friendship started.

Tarisai then recollected the bad things that had happened to her, including the suspension from that school from which she then transferred. The girls left, and I made it clear to her that not everyone liked everyone, including herself. "Don't forget how Emma and crew plotted against your grandmother, Eti, young as they all were."

Even in her last school, she had more enemies than friends. Maybe that's why she immersed herself in figures and thermodynamics. The precision and predictability of equations seemed to offer her solace amidst the chaos of social dynamics. Yet for her religious dynamics, there was so much entropy and disequilibrium.

"Yes mother." With that she went to the spare room and buried her head in Shakespeare collection. I knew that would take her to sleep. But I had a brief chat with her. I didn't want to upset her with any melancholy so I changed the subject. Besides, it was her birthday in three days, and I had the perfect gift. Two weeks earlier, back at the village, I had helped the sister-in-charge spring clean her house to make room for new staff. She paid me well and allowed me to carry along whatever I fancied from the clutter. Among the treasures was what the sister-in-charge called a harmonica. Immediately, I knew Tarisai would love this addition to her instrument collection. I also brought along the leaflet with basic instructions on use and cleaning. Her Uncle Mhasvi had already given Tarisai a *chipendani*, and she was getting better at playing it.

As my daughter delved into the pages of her favourite subject, she paused and talked about the third law of thermodynamics—how it states that as the temperature of a system approaches absolute zero, the entropy of the system approaches a minimum value. That moment, I understood her language. She often shared her jargon, and I could relate to some of the principles. Inertia, for example, was my favourite and easiest definition to understand—it's the tendency of an object to remain at rest or in motion unless acted upon by an external force. Anyway, I knew then that in my daughter's world, amidst the fluctuations of emotions and uncertainties, she found her own version of 'absolute zero'—a place of tranquillity and order where entropy was minimised, and her mind could find peace.

"Mother," she said softly, glancing up from her book, "You know how in thermodynamics, they talk about entropy and chaos right? Well, it's like when everything around me feels chaotic, diving into Shakespeare's world is like reaching that state of minimum entropy. It's where everything just makes sense, and I can find peace. But above all, my Bible here, says 'May the peace of the Lord, which transcends all understanding, be with you always.'" With that I nodded, smiled and closed her door.

Chapter 16

Tarisai outgrew the family custom of sharing toothbrushes. One family, one tooth. I established this to unify the family and to discourage Tarisai from picky. If this was too excessive, she wouldn't fit in other environments away from home, so I shad to train her. Her first toothbrush was rightly for toddlers and after that phase, she graduated into the adult toothbrush world. At least that's what I made her to believe as the reason for sharing. Only I knew the true reason, I wanted to get as close to my husband as possible. He had a tendency of befriending my friends more than their partners. He often displayed a level of sociability that made me uncomfortable. I wasn't possessive, just obsessive. It troubled me, and despite discussing this issue with him repeatedly, his response remained unchanged. Perhaps it was due to his name, Tazivei, that he seemed so naive, unassuming, and clueless. Women could be cunning, yet it seemed as though he didn't realise how handsome and fetching, he was. People like Marujata and her daughters were offering physical relief and gratification to men in the mining town of Kindu. I couldn't just sit idly by and pray like Tarisai did, while predators like Marujata roamed freely, preying on our husbands. Even her sons were up to no good. One was picking pockets at Mbare Musika, while another was targeting drunk miners on payday. This is why I sympathised with

Mangondi's wife. Many women were drawn to her husband for his exceptional drumming skills and apparent masculinity. There were other equally skilled drummers, but he surpassed them all in popularity. Even though there was no evidence of infidelity, the mere thought unsettled me.

* * *

All the while as Mangondi focused on the drum, Nancy focused on his strong hands, his broad shoulders and the mop of hair on his head. She secretly knew his drumming schedules and any ad hoc events. She also made excuses to attend these in disguise as she was the white farmer's wife. She would certainly be out of place and her husband would be angered knowing that she was mingling with commoners. Moreover, the local headman was a sworn enemy of the whites and would not allow any of them to attend their gatherings. Hence, there was no way she could openly enjoy the drumming. His hatred was so intense that whenever there was a dance night, he would attend accompanied by his eldest son an engineering hopeful who was in his late twenties and still not married. They never missed any gathering. Rumour had it that his father loathed the whites because they were responsible for his wife's death. She fell off a tractor driven by the farmer and the injury was fatal she didn't make it to the clinic.

* * *

Mangondi's wife is the one who made everyone at home dislike yellow rice. The curry and turmeric choked the life out of you as it simmered worse when eating. It was nauseating. There was always plenty of leftovers which would eventually be fed to the hens. Others rinse off the turmeric after boiling whereas others simply add a few dashes not shovels of turmeric and curry. She was told but being the person she was, she rubbished it off. She was a know-it-all type of woman. She was distasteful.

Another distasteful one in the family was Uncle Mike's wife. It was so hilarious when aunty Sanelisiwe said that she was the one who taught Uncle Mike about grooming once they were married. In life those people who just want to be said they have said something, they need accreditation, they need to be credited that they throw themselves at everyone as their saviour. Growing up, Uncle Mike was known for his cologne collection which he layered from roll on, lotion, after shave and the eau de perfume. A pour home. In contrast to Sanelisiwe shouting to the world that she transformed him into the classy man that he was today. The whole group gathered in her kitchen couldn't hide their chuckles when she claimed that before they were together, Uncle Mike only applied roll on and nothing more and he was so ignorant and incognisant of general rules of etiquette be it telephone, dining etiquette or general courtesy. Only her upbringing was excellent and on point worthy to be signposted as a benchmark. Well life would be boring if all humans lived the same way. One lady snapped back when she tried to teach her what sparkling water was and how to drink it.

The lady said, "Well missy, apart from sparkling water, I also take flavoured water. Now, are you going to advise me what flavour is best and how I should hold the bottle and take one sip at a time and not gobble?" Aunt Sanelisiwe's lips parted, but no words came out. Instead, her shoulders slumped, a silent admission of defeat. She also assumed that if something was new to her, it was new to everyone else. In her arrogance, she remained blinded by her own ignorance.

Such narrow-mindedness was surprising for a woman of her self-assured flair.

Never mind his wife, Uncle Mike was a favourite of mine. He had a refreshing attitude towards life—never judgmental, especially when it came to enjoying a good beer. He wouldn't judge you for drinking beer, as long as you didn't do anything stupid like singing your mother's name. His appreciation for my specially brewed beer matched his taste for fine wines and other rich palettes cultivated during his international travels. He graciously introduced me to the world of wine, and to my uncultured palate, most of the wines were good. His timing couldn't have been better. It was during a time of economic turmoil in the late 1980s and early 1990s when Zimbabwe faced economic challenges that led to the implementation of the Economic Structural Adjustment Program (ESAP). This program aimed to address these issues by making changes to how the economy worked, making it easier for businesses to operate, and reducing government intervention. We ate yellow *sadza*, a departure from the usual white *sadza* my children preferred, which was becoming increasingly scarce due to the hardships. With maize in short supply and our silos empty, the nation relied on international to survive. Uncle Mike mentioned that in countries like Italy, this yellow cornmeal made polenta and is considered a delicacy, prepared in a way different from our *sadza*. While it tasted raw to some, it wasn't necessarily awful. Some referred to it as Kenyan maize meal, leading Tarisai to believe that Kenya meant yellow. Apparently, yellow maize meal was more common in Kenya hence the nickname. Those were the harsh days of ESAP and having a meal a day was enough. Most parents who always ensured children had new clothes for Christmas were at a loss that time, such that getting second-hand clothes was a bonus.

Against this backdrop, I vividly recall the Christmas of 1991 when Uncle Mike brought a bottle of chateau, sparking a buzz throughout the village. Despite the challenges we faced, Uncle Mike's gesture brought a sense of joy and festivity to our community, reminding us to cherish moments of happiness amidst adversity. As customary, we had gathered for Christmas, with even Kindu quiet as many workers had returned to their hometowns. That day at the growth point, Uncle Mike stole the show with his chateau, overshadowing the boasts of those with their green and brown bottled beers. Everyone clamoured for a sip of the chateau, though Uncle Mike insisted it was not for communal sharing like our traditional beer pots. He was quite particular, emphasising that it wasn't meant for passing mouth to mouth as we did with our customary beer pots. It was a drink for those of refined taste, he declared. Reluctantly, we passed the cup around, each taking a sip in turn. Those were merry times.

Nowadays, I hear you can be arrested for public drinking if the police catch you enjoying a drink at the shops. Sharing the same gourd was better, as the chances of being poisoned were low; the culprit could end up drinking their own poison or ensnaring innocent bystanders in the crossfire. The danger with these selfish single-person drinks lay in the potential for them to be laced with crocodile bile, hidden beneath a long fingernail. That's why I always discouraged my husband from growing his nails, unlike most men. In any investigation, those with long nails were the prime suspects, whether they were present on the day or not.

Looking back to the mid-90s, around 1996, with the advent of better technology like VCRs, I approached Uncle Mike with a huge request. Over the years, I began to understand the depth of my daughter Tari's sincerity and conviction in her faith, and I felt guilty for deceiving her about the cub. While I knew it was eventually rescued, I wasn't entirely certain about the details. I knew Uncle Mike had access to higher offices worldwide. In 1980, I heard a rumour that he declined to have his face featured on the sixpence. Perhaps it was just a fable, but with Uncle Mike, one could never be certain. His neutral and non-judgmental nature made me share my plea with him. A beloved uncle known to host regular family gatherings, and also known for imparting wisdom and engaging in thought-provoking discussions with his nieces and nephews. His advocacy for education and encouragement for everyone to pursue their passions and dreams also made him the ideal person to share my plea with. Above all, I knew he would not share this revelation-cum-confession with his nosy wife Sanelisiwe. With her desire to control her husband, I knew she might have convinced him to ditch my request as a waste of time and resources. Instead of some of us harmless congenial people, this is one person whom Tarisai needed to convert to Christianity. Perhaps that would tame her distasteful ways and make her a submissive wife and meek person in general. She was such a turn-off that if it were in my netball days, I'd mark her throughout the game, whether she had the ball or not.

Uncle Mike played the VCR showing a video that the cub was indeed taken care of, fully recovered, and integrated into a zoo in Santa Rosa before being reunited with its family back in the wild. Uncle Mike, with his well-travelled and knowledgeable background, was the perfect person to approach for this. After watching the video, Tarisai's eyes sparkled with joy, her smile stretching from ear to ear as she turned to me and uncle, expressing her gratitude. As she spoke, her voice trembled with excitement and relief. Meanwhile, a surge of warmth flooded through me, a weight lifted off my shoulders as I basked in the tranquillity of knowing that the matter was settled for good. My heart danced with ecstasy, its rhythm matching the joy pulsating through the room. This called for a celebration, and rightly so. We clinked glasses, the crisp aroma of wine mingling with the laughter and chatter filling the room. Tarisai opted for the humble *korowota* (a mixture of sugar and cool water), her smile radiant.

Chapter 17

No one suspected the headman of having an extra marital affair. He was a role model for many youths. However, I had my doubts especially with the way he jibed with Sharai. It shouted seduction. I am still puzzled as to why most people failed to notice. I remember at one time he shouted at some drunken men who kept making lewd comments on women performing the *Jerusarema* dance (traditional fertility dance). He told them to learn to tame their salacity. From that day onwards, he earned the nickname, Sala. Salacity was a word he learnt while in training at the neighbouring monastery in Makumbe. One would be inclined the Benedictine monks there instilled in him strong principles and morals. But, well, men will always be men. It seemed he only learnt Latin, " *ego te salutamus*" (we greet you).

Anyway, there were rumours that some of the priests were causing subtle havoc in the villages. Tarisai tried to explain the priests' vow to chastity and why they choose never to marry, but I still struggled to understand. What I do know and understand is that everyone has their own path. "Everyone has the gift of free will," Tarisai and her pastor explained to me several times, but I failed to comprehend it all. It was like trying to grasp Tarisai's Jacobian matrices or the laws of thermodynamics, which she loved so much. Each sunrise painted the sky with hues of gold and crimson, heralding a new day filled with a chorus of questions that echoed in the depths of my soul. And as the sun dipped below the horizon, casting long shadows across the land, a silent plea for understanding whispered through the evening breeze. How does one reconcile the soaring hymnals of Christianity with the primal resonance of ancestral voices, woven deep into the fabric of our existence? How does one honour the sacred traditions of kin while kneeling at the altar of a singular God? Once again, Tarisai explained, "There is the perfect will of God and then the permissive will of God. No one is really forced. It means God has a specific plan for your life, but we can always choose otherwise. But mother, have you ever wondered what would have happened if Grandmother had rejected her calling? Did she have the option to refuse in the first place? How was she chosen?" I told her she could ask her father; I was too tired for such a deep conversation.

Well, there were ancestral dance ceremonies like the bira, which involved singing, drumming, and trance-like dancing, serving as a way to communicate with ancestral spirits and seek their guidance. These dances played a vital role in our local culture, serving as expressions of identity, storytelling, and community cohesion. One fine day in the lovely peaceful village of Mara Valley, the air was filled with anticipation as the community prepared for a grand celebration. The occasion was both a harvest festival and a spiritual gathering, merging the joy of abundance with reverence for the ancestors. As the sun dipped low in the sky, the rhythmic beats of the drums echoed through the village. A special group of dancers emerged, adorned in colourful attire with beads and feathers, gathered at the centre of the village square. Among them was Mangondi the charming daring drummer. A man of agility and exuberance. Mangondi announced, pouring some beer on the ground, "Today, we honour the spirit of strength and vitality through this event. Let our movements echo the resilience of our people." Ululations followed by heavy clapping filled the air as the dancers launched into a spirited performance. Their feet moved in perfect sync with the driving rhythm of the drums. Jumps, spins, and rhythmic stomps filled the air as some villagers joined and others gathered to watch in awe.

As night fell, the atmosphere shifted to a more solemn tone. The villagers gathered around a sacred fire, and the melodies of the *mbira* resonated in the air. The ceremony commenced, led by Mbuya Zvirevo, her eyes reflecting a deep connection to the spiritual realm. She started chanting, "Ancestors, hear our voices. Bless this harvest and guide us with your wisdom."

Mbuya Zvirevo continued her rhythmic chanting, creating a spiritual harmony that seemed to transcend the earthly realm. As the intensity of the ceremony heightened, some participants entered a trance-like state, embodying the presence of ancestral spirits. This ceremony served as a bridge between the tangible and the spiritual, a moment where the community sought guidance and blessings for the future. This was precisely where Tarisai and Eti clashed. On most other matters, they found harmony, except when it came to seeking guidance from the ancestors, those who had gone before us to join their forefathers. Tarisai pointed to her Bible, saying, "The dead know nothing; do not enquire of the dead."

Tarisai's pastor explained to me that the issue was the strong emphasis on communicating with ancestral spirits and seeking their guidance. Some branches of Christianity discourage practices that involve what may be perceived as worshiping or communicating with entities other than the

Christian God, but others allow it. I know that scholars and other so-called wise people may argue that the blending of indigenous spiritual practices with Christian rituals, which sometimes occurs in syncretic contexts, can be seen as diluting or compromising Christian beliefs. Tarisai remained firm in her stance that water and oil never mix and that was her view on those two beliefs. It bothered her that members of her own family including me, practise a blend of indigenous spiritual beliefs inherited from our ancestors and Christian practices introduced by missionaries decades ago. Vasco da Gama is the name that resonated among us as we were taught about the arrival of missionaries. Look at Tarisai, she may deny all she wants. She's a mirror image of Eti. They both enjoy singing but in parallel dimensions. One is in a séance and the other in a trance. These are some of the nuances of life, of faith. I love my mother. I love my daughter, yet I somewhat have to choose my loyalty to one of them. Tarisai says you cannot serve both God and mammon. Mbuya Zvirevo says how did our fathers exist before Vasco da Gama converted them. Similar to how the children of Israel received manna from heaven while in the wilderness or desert, we also received food under *muhacha* (Parinari curatellifolia) trees.

Part of our community's customs and traditions included ceremonies where prayers to ancestral spirits are recited alongside Christian hymns. At one time Tarisai's eyes almost popped out during a harvest festival when she observed a crowd making traditional offerings to their ancestors for a bountiful harvest, followed by a Christian thanksgiving service led by a clergyman. There were others too, like her, who adhered strictly to Christian doctrine. They argued that the blending of indigenous practices with Christian rituals diluted the purity of their faith and compromised their relationship with God. Then there were those who said the traditional practices were part of their heritage, while others categorically refused to tarnish their cultural and spiritual beliefs with Christian ones. It was a case of morality versus expedience and whether right or wrong depended on who fed your stomach.

Not only for Tarisai, but for me too, this conflict became a central theme in her journey as she grappled with questions of cultural identity, faith, loyalty and belonging. As she navigated the tensions between tradition and modernity, Tarisai had to reconcile the syncretic nature of the general beliefs with her own understanding of Christianity and spirituality. I also had to understand where I stood in my role as a daughter to a spirit medium and mother to a girl with a Christian calling. Apart from the biology, the only single strongest element that bound us all three was respect for each other.

What I failed to understand was why there was so much division among Tarisai's kind. It was important to note that interpretations of religious practices could vary widely among individuals, and different Christian denominations might have varying perspectives on cultural traditions. Some Christians might actively participate in traditional ceremonies while maintaining their Christian faith, viewing these practices as a way of connecting with their cultural heritage. But where did we draw the line, and who drew it if not the individual? What I came to understand is that, in essence, some religious traditional ceremonies contradicted teachings of the Bible, and this was subjective and dependent on one's theological beliefs and interpretation of scripture. People within the same community or family might have diverse views on the compatibility of traditional practices with their Christian faith or traditional religion. Tolerance. Unity. Peace. Harmony. Love. Understanding.

A *bira* (ancestral ceremony) was held one time. Under the moonlit sky in our cosy village, my family gathered around the flickering flames of the sacred fire for the ceremony. The air was thick with the mesmerising sounds of the *mbira* and the rhythmic chanting. Other spirit mediums led the ceremony with reverence, while Tarisai, watched with a furrowed brow, her Bible in hand. She whispered to her sister Zivai, "I understand the importance of tradition, but I can't shake the feeling that this goes against my Christian beliefs."

I chimed in knowing Zivai might not have the perfect answer as Tarisai could be a little intense in her convictions. I told her that it connected us to our ancestors and that it was part of who we are.

Immediately Tarisai flipped through the Bible. "But the Bible warns against communicating with spirits. In Corinthians 10:20-21, it says, "No, I imply that what pagans sacrifice they offer to demons and not to God. I do not want you to be participants with demons. You cannot drink the cup of the Lord and the cup of demons."

I sighed and shrugged my shoulders as I answered. "I respect your beliefs, Tari. But for us, this is about honouring our ancestors and seeking guidance. It's for reverence."

Tarisai enjoyed debate at times. I don't even know why she brought the same topic now and again. She opened her Bible again, "We are to worship the one true God, not intermediaries. In 1 Timothy 2:5, it says, 'For there is one God, and there is one mediator between God and men, the man Christ Jesus.'"

I was not backing down fast either. She was on our ground so I had to give her a sit. "I see your point, but this a way of connecting with our past, our roots. Remember how we lived before the missionaries came? You know those are not fables. We also received manna just in a localised form."

"I also value our traditions, mother, but we must be careful not to mix practices that may conflict with our faith. You know I only come here out of respect for grandmother. I will not compromise on my faith with what I do not understand."

As the ceremony continued, the crackling fire cast shadows on peoples' faces, emphasising the contrast between the ancient rituals of the *bira* and the teachings within the pages of Tarisai's Bible. In that moment, the village echoed with the harmonies of tradition and spirituality, leaving the Tarisai, her mother and her sister with a shared but unspoken understanding of the delicate balance they sought to maintain.

Chapter 18

My daughter Tarisai, troubled me with her engineering studies, how she always passionately delved into the complexities of Euler equations and Jacobian matrices. When she explained, her eyes sparkled with excitement as she describing how these mathematical concepts unveil the secrets of the physical world. She walked you through a journey of numbers and figures, not of women but of intrigue and enigma. Deep down I was proud of her but she took it too far.

"Mom, Dad, Euler's formula is like magic! It connects complex numbers, trigonometry, and even imaginary units into this elegant equation." Whenever she said "dad" I knew she was up to something.

My husband and I exchanged bemused glances, recognising our daughter's intellectual fervour. However, it was becoming too much. One morning I walked into the kitchen to find my daughter applying Euler's equation to the coffee brewing process, discussing the angles and rotations involved.

"You see, mother, it's all about understanding the dynamic flow of fluids. Euler's equation helps optimise the coffee extraction," she said smiling.

I held a puzzled expression, glanced at my husband, who raised an eyebrow in response. That same afternoon, in the garden, I saw Tarisai meticulously sketching Jacobian matrices in the soil, explaining how they represent the interconnectedness of the plants. She quickly added, "You see, the Jacobian matrix helps us understand how changes in one variable affect others. It's like optimising the growth of our garden."

I was not thrilled at all and so was my husband. On realising that our daughter's engineering enthusiasm was seeping into every aspect of our daily lives, we shuddered.

That evening we discussed how fascinating it was that she applied engineering to everything, but sometimes it felt like our daily lives were turning into a mathematical experiment.

"I appreciate her passion, but there's a fine line between enthusiasm and… well, turning our home into an engineering lab." My husband for once agreed with me. He always sided with her irrationally.

We sat her down after supper. I started. "Sweetheart, we love your passion for engineering, but let's also enjoy the simplicity of life without turning everything into a mathematical equation. In the olden days, our fathers would give thanks and praise around the *muhacha* tree and food would appear. If they were hungry, not when they wanted to test the theory, or you want to call it myth. He who was truly hungry and in need of food would be fed. Is that equivalent of manna? I don't know. All I know is the food would be piping hot and it could be a rapoko meal in wooden plates. You eat, you leave leftovers there, if any. Most times because the food was so delicious and being hungry, one would finish it all. Even the plate wouldn't need cleaning." We all laughed.

Tarisai quickly asked, eyes beaming with fascination, "Where did the plates go? How come it doesn't happen anymore? What changed?"

"The same way they appeared, that's how they would disappear. Well, my dear, listen, we were foretold that these occurrences, feats would end when we abandon our culture and blend it with foreign ones."

Tarisai leaned back in her seat against the wall, even more puzzled and said, "Is that not discrimination? We are a global village. Look at how the Red Cross takes people from across the world to help those in need in diverse places and environs. Even, our Uncle Mike here, he goes about the world, not in eighty days ha-ha, but all over, for a job that gives medicine to anyone anywhere. I see nothing wrong with that." My nodded. I somewhat had similar questions to Tarisai, was that equivalent to manna? There were significant similarities yet so parallel in these two sets of faith. Tarisai explained at one point that the Bible says one should either be hot or cold and not lukewarm. Its either you are in or you are out, no in between. Was that practical though? Where does one draw the line? Mr Winston said it was like cheating on your partner, one leg inside the house and one leg outside, there is no half cheating.

As Tarisai discussed with us, she realised there were numerous complexities in life that made her question certain doctrines and societal expectations especially gender roles. We then addressed our original concern, the 'mathefication' of our house, and redirected her to pursuing accounting since she liked numbers, and she went berserk.

"The times have changed, I can't study accounting simply because it's the 'have-to' course," Tarisai said looking straight into her father's eyes. He looked away shaking his head.

"I'm not crazy. It's my love for math, for numbers. I talk math, I eat math, so it's easy and natural to apply it in my daily life," she sighed as she finished.

Tarisai's father shook his head again clutching his forehead which resembled that of a primate.

"You too? You both think I am insane? How absurd!" Tarisai paced the room with one hand gripping her hair while the other waved involuntarily. Tarisai often avoided extreme use of gestures as she complained that instead of emphasising or adding clarity, they destructed the listener. It is on rare occasions when irate that she found her arms flying around. She gripped her braids to control the unwarranted movement of her arms.

Her father was the last person she expected to discourage her from numbers. From the days of the leopard cub, I had finally reached an amicable agreement with her by taking her to Njanja. Perhaps it would work again. I nudged my husband but he remained quiet and fixated at the ceiling. I stamped my foot and he nodded at me taking the cue.

"Tari, listen we —" he spoke in a soft voice.

"Father, I'm hurt, so disappointed beyond words. I thought you wanted the best for me always," she whimpered, staring at her feet.

"Why don't we return to Njanja, maybe the change of scenery will invoke some exciting inspiration," her father coaxed.

Tarisai rolled her eyes facing sideways. She knew well enough not to disrespect her dad, no matter how furious she was.

At this point, I knew it was in everyone's best interests that I held my tongue. My husband stood by our daughter even when I reprimanded her. So, for her, his reaction and sentiments were a huge blow. Even that phase when she obsessed over black clothes and refused pink clothes, he saw nothing wrong with that. He said let her be, she's still growing. While this was an uncomfortable situation for us, I smiled inwardly that he was finally stamping his authority as the man of the house. For many years, she was ever right in his eyes. Always. However, I felt sad seeing my daughter so dejected with her shoulders drooped and staring on the floor. Usually, she talked with her head held high almost touching the clouds. This situation had to be resolved today for the sake of sanity.

"Euler's Identity, I ,we understand but this? This Jacobian Matrix you have introduced just complicates the situation. It's not healthy for your psyche. Don't you see? Njanja may be the magic equation, how about that?" Her dad continued.

Tarisai snapped clutching her temples, "No that's not it, please, I need to be alone! I want to see Uncle Mike. Let me go and see my uncle. He will understand."

Mike was a grandson to the last boy in mother's family. He was Sekuru Tinzi's grandson. He was a well-off and knowledgeable uncle working as an executive in a multinational pharmaceutical company called Benson Labs which often saw him around the globe. Born into a family of inquisitive and daring people, he was exposed to a wide range of topics and opportunities from a young age. Sekuru Tinzi instilled in him and all his other siblings, a strong sense of curiosity and a passion for learning. It's on this background and his history of being objective that Tarisai knew he would side with her. Once he took your side, that was a certain victory. Everyone would agree even though begrudgingly.

Uncle Mike had a flair about him that whispered class and sophistication. Despite being in his mid-40s, he commanded respect from across older generations. He respected people too. During the week, he would be immaculately dressed in bespoke suits and well-polished shoes. Come weekend, he would be clad in shorts and airy t-shirts or some neutral-coloured shirts with aviators. Tarisai liked his dressing sense as much as she liked his objectiveness. Whether right or wrong, he had a knack for laying out the facts plainly and leaving it up to the individual to make their own decisions.

Known among his friends and family as a walking encyclopaedia, Mike was well-versed in a wide array of subjects, ranging from biology and chemistry to history and fine arts. It was his insatiable thirst for knowledge that made him the go-to person for advice and information among both family and peers alike. Most relatives including me, crossed fingers so Uncle Mike wouldn't marry fearing that a wife might change him into someone unapproachable, distant from family gatherings. However, fate had other plans. Uncle Mike found his perfect match in Aunty Sanelisiwe, a woman who complemented his life in most ways. Aunty Sanelisiwe was not only an accomplished florist but also a woman of intellect and passion. Despite dropping out of nursing school, she possessed a deep love for learning and a keen interest in nature and travel. It was during their college years that Uncle Mike and Aunty Sanelisiwe first met, bonding over their shared love for nature, travelling and intellectual pursuits despite coming from different social backgrounds.

Uncle Mike was a doting uncle who took a keen interest in the lives of his nieces and nephews. He provided guidance and mentorship, helping them excel academically and in their career pursuits. Mike attended prestigious universities, earning degrees in both business and engineering, which laid the foundation for his career. He started as an entry-level employee in the multinational company and steadily climbed the corporate ladder through his dedication, intelligence, and problem-solving skills. She knew he would find reason and make them understand to let her make her own choices.

Chapter 19

A knock on the ajar door broke Tarisai's reverie. "You could have just walked in, seeing the door wasn't closed," Tarisai sulked, gritting her teeth. Tikana grabbed her chin, tilting her face up to match his eye gaze. Her dreamy eyes followed his, like a sheep led to the slaughter

"I know you mean well, but aren't you taking this a little too far?" His icy breath enveloped Tarisai's forehead, which resembled the face of a bus. She waited for him to finish, as was his custom: speak, pause, and stare. Meanwhile, he sipped his Tarino with one hand, holding Tarisai by the left shoulder. "In your search for truth and deeper meaning, you have isolated yourself. Short of a better phrase, I would say you are an alienated moving being. All you do is read and meditate, as you call it—"

"It's studying the Bible, not just reading. You copy that!" Tarisai insisted, pushing him off with her index finger in a matter-of- fact manner. He adjusted himself, his expression momentarily disrupted by Tarisai's push.

"Let me finish, don't hush me," he whispered squeezing her pale hand." He savoured his Tarino before tossing the bottle onto the sofa making Tarisai roll her eyes. He was usually meticulous and would never litter unless agitated or under unusual circumstances.

He resumed, "I know you're not reading baboon and hare folklore. It's important, and I respect that, but you've stopped living." His eyes scanned the room before he turned around, hands still tucked into his back pockets. He bowed his head, shaking it. Attempting to speak, he gasped, then ran his lean fingers through his thick locks, resembling triangular logs. His once stern gaze softened, now pleading. Taking a step forward, he paused, observing her expression, which had mellowed since he released her hand. The defiance in her eyes had vanished. She nodded followed by a quick glance at the 'blank painting'. She referred to it as the painting of purpose. It is through this painting that she reinforced her belief in her destiny, referring to herself as the blessed one. The painting was a square, almost the length of a ruler, in a pastel yellow which faded into a soft white. Although appearing empty, devoid of any visible markings, it held a myriad of profound meanings for her, offering perspectives ranging from inspiration to mathematical exploration. According to her, yellow symbolised creation and white represented expiration. Together, they showed both nothingness and the universe, signifying the cycle of creation and dissolution. Indeed, the painting stood at the intersection of indecision and resolution.

Tarisai tuned towards him and said, "The only time I will date you is when you ditch your habit of pinching yourself from the back pockets," she looked away, tilting her head and hiding a subtle smile. This proved to be a perpetual point of difference as neither party budged from their opinion.

"Countless times, I have explained that pinching myself is a reflex."

"Placing your hefty palms in your small back pockets and then, just listen, pinching yourself, that's pure reflex? Come on, don't be ridiculous. It is so annoying. I could never stand it."

"Maybe it's my way of ensuring I'm not dreaming," he retorted with a smirk, attempting to lighten the mood.

Tarisai rolled her eyes, unconvinced. "Dreaming? More like testing your pain tolerance, if you ask me."

He chuckled and winked. "Well, you know what they say, 'No pain, no gain.'"

"Right, because gaining a date with me is totally worth the pain," she replied, though a hint of amusement danced in her eyes.

"Absolutely," he replied, flashing a charming grin. "And who knows, maybe one day you'll find my quirky habits endearing."

Tarisai shook her head, still wearing a teasing smile. "Don't hold your breath on that one."

Tikana's expression shifted, his tone becoming more serious as he returned to the earlier concern about the Bible. "But seriously, Tarisai, I worry about you. It's not just about the Bible; it's about you losing touch with the world around you. You're so focused on this one thing that you're missing out on life."

Tarisai's smile faded, replaced by a thoughtful expression. "I appreciate your concern, but this is important to me. It's not just about studying the Bible; it's about finding purpose and meaning."

He nodded, while scratching his head. "I get that, I do. But there's more to life than just one book. I just don't want to see you miss out on everything else." Taking a deep breath, he added, "And, well, I want to spend more time with you. You know, as a boyfriend, not just a friend. But it's hard when you're so... consumed by this."

Tarisai's eyes widened at his unexpected admission, her lips parting slightly as if to speak, yet no words escaped. A subtle flush crept up her cheeks, betraying the emotions swirling within her. She glanced away, her gaze drifting to a distant point.

After a moment of silence, she turned back to him, her expression softening. "I... I didn't realise," she began slowly, her voice laced with uncertainty. "Our friendship means so much to me, and I don't want to jeopardise that. But..." She paused, her eyes meeting his with a mixture of hesitance and curiosity. "But perhaps there's something more between us," she continued, her voice gaining confidence. "I just need some time to sort through my feelings." A tentative smile graced her lips, revealing the vulnerability beneath her words.

After Tikana left, Olivia crept in, and Tarisai sighed with relief upon seeing that it was her friend who had returned. They had been chatting earlier before the young man interrupted.

Being the headman's son, Tikana often had numerous girls throwing themselves at him. The moment I saw him casting his nets towards my dear Tarisai, I stalked him like a fish eagle. Already, I had my doubts about his father, the headman. I had an inkling about him, yet no evidence to pin him down. My husband always chided me, saying it was none of my business what the headman did in his extracurricular activities, as long as he led the village with fairness and distributed seeds in ample time for the rains.

* * *

As Nancy continued her clandestine English lessons with the headman's son, the threads of connection in the village became even more entangled. The rhythmic dance of secrecy extended beyond Mara Valley and Nancy, weaving a complex tapestry of relationships. Whispers of suspicion grew louder, fuelled by the sight of Nancy spending time not only with Tikana but also with the headman's family. Mbuya Nandi, the village gossip, keenly observed these interactions and began connecting the dots.

Whenever Nancy and the headman met, their eyes would lock briefly, a silent exchange passing between them, laden with unspoken truths and hidden desires. In that moment, time seemed to stand still, the world around them fading into insignificance as they locked gazes. No words were needed; the shared understanding between them spoke volumes, a language all their own. Their stolen moment, though fleeting, felt infinite in its significance. In the midst of the mundane routines of everyday life, they found solace in each other's company, a brief respite from the constraints of reality.

One day, as the drumming party echoed through the village, Mbuya Nandi cornered Nancy, "Teaching the headman's son English now, are we? It seems your influence knows no bounds."

Nancy, caught off guard, stammered, "It's just language lessons, Mbuya Nandi. Education knows no boundaries."

Mbuya Nandi, however, raised an eyebrow, "In a village where secrets are as prevalent as the dust on our paths, one must be cautious, especially when walking on the edge of multiple roads."

Many things went unnoticed in our village now that I think of it. Nancy once approached me requesting to learn the mesmerising *Jerusarema* dance. I explained to her, "Jerusarema is a dance of our ancestors, a dance that tells stories of our people. To learn, you must feel the rhythm deep within your soul."

Nancy then eagerly stepped closer, her eyes fixed on my gestures. I raised my hands then continued, "It begins with the heartbeat of the drums. Listen closely, feel the pulse, and let your body respond." She nodded saying she would do her best. I showed her how she had to sway your hips fast enough to match the tempo of the drums. It was a dance where you let the energy flow from the earth through your feet. Nancy stumbled at first, but with determination, she began to find her rhythm. As the night unfolded, the village gathered for *pfonda* with the various dances creating a rhythmic symphony that resonated through the land. In spite of Nancy a rarely attending *pfondas* she appreciated well my effort in an attempt to teach her. In the midst of embracing the ancient tradition of the Jerusarema dance, Nancy spoke passionately about the profound sense of belonging she felt, describing it as more than just a dance but a timeless expression of culture and unity. Her words were accompanied by a radiant smile that seemed to emanate from her eyes. However, at the time, I was unaware of Nancy's true intentions. She had ulterior motives for learning the dance – to engage in an affair with her married boyfriend. Had I known, I would have refused to fulfil her request, as I do not support infidelity.

What business did I have in monitoring other people's homes when I had my own pressing issues like, encouraging Tarisai to consider marriage in future, or to help her maintain proper traditional courtesy. I might have succeeded in most maternal roles or domestic duties, but taming Tarisai with basic rules of speaking one at a time wasn't my forte. For instance, I successfully cared for her using traditional methods such as fortifying her with medicinal herbs and feeding her by pre-chewing food to make it easier for her to consume. I also employed traditional techniques like using my mouth to clear mucus from her small nose, and on some occasions, even using diluted soap solutions to help relieve constipation.

My struggle to tame her was a long lost one. "Tari," I said, "you need to understand that when someone calls, you should let them speak first. They called you, so they have something to say. If you had so much to speak, you should have called them first. The moment someone says hello, you—the receiver—start yelping. That's just basic etiquette. I may not know much about technology, but this is general knowledge. It's even embedded in our genealogy." Tarisai grinned as if caught offside. It was easy for her to remember her Euler and them, but not simple stuff like this.

Interrupting others while they are speaking is considered rude. Eti had mastered the art of giving others the chance to speak, even while she was talking. It was a skill not everyone possessed. When she spoke in her shoes as Mbuya Zvirevo, no one interrupted. But Tarisai seemed obstinate about it. During a silly heated discussion with her friend Olivia, I snapped, "The two of you continue talking, but who's listening now? What's the use of all this chatter if no one's truly listening? It's like speaking into the wind, heard but not understood. Talking over each other only muddles the conversation, missing the essence of what's being said.

Perhaps what truly annoyed me was their squabble over the headman's son, Tarisai's perennial boyfriend. The way his father wore his belt above his waist had left me bewildered. Why should the children bear the burden of their fathers' actions? Well, why should children suffer for the sins of their fathers? Even Tarisai's Bible says, "the children will suffer for the fathers' sins up to the third generation." Yet, later promised liberation. "The one who eats sour grapes will have his own teeth set on edge," I reminded myself not to meddle in their affairs, to let them bicker and banter as they pleased, but just one at a time. After all, imagine a teacher trying to make sense of 45 students all clamouring for attention simultaneously. It would be pure chaos, wouldn't it? I left them but stood at the door, eavesdropping. Sometimes, I just couldn't resist my curiosity about trivial romances. I heard that boy had cheated and he claimed he had been trapped.

"You still love him?" Olivia nudged her by the elbow almost tipping her off balance as she looked in the distance.

Masking a subtle smile, Tarisai squeezed Olivia's hand. In an instant, they burst into laughter. Tarisai then quoted scripture, "It is said He has not given us a spirit of timidity but of power of love and of a sound mind. Where there is confusion, that's not God. It is written God is not the author of confusion. I am confused. I love him, I don't love him. I don't know." She hid her face in her palms.

"I was better off alone, and this handsome, humble hunk took me on a serenade. I swayed along, basking in the apparent glory of love. This distracted me to the point of losing touch with my precious worship moments." Tarisai chuckled, her tone tinged with sarcasm, which made Olivia raise her eyebrows. She knew when her friend was being sarcastic and when she wasn't.

Tarisai jumped onto her bed and lay on her back. This was her sign of surrender, letting go, and letting God take charge—a moment of absolute relaxation, believing that all troubles were in God's hands. It was this conviction that energized her amidst troubles sometimes. However, as she landed on the bed, a mirror sitting on the edge bounced off and shattered.

Although both girls shunned superstition, they struggled to ignore certain beliefs. Breaking a mirror topped their list, followed by sweeping oneself or being swept with a broom. Surely, this broken mirror signalled a bad omen. Superstition aside, they both observed that an unfortunate event always seemed to follow breaking a mirror. Then again, Tarisai claimed to live by faith and not by sight. She knew she ought not to entertain such beliefs.

Startled, Tarisai leaped to her feet while Olivia gathered the splinters. After cleaning up Olivia, with her fond knowledge of language, continued. "Tarisai, do you agree that the study of literature leads to a growth of intelligence and sensibility?"

"Yes, I agree. The study of literature can indeed lead to a growth of intelligence and sensibility. Literature exposes readers to a wide range of human experiences, perspectives, and emotions, fostering empathy and understanding. Analysing complex texts requires critical thinking skills, promoting intellectual development."

"So, my point is, literature often deals with profound themes and ideas, encouraging readers to reflect deeply on life, society, and the human condition. Overall, engaging with literature can enhance cognitive abilities, emotional intelligence, and cultural awareness. But this guy, Tikana, he doesn't want the emotional attachment that comes with being in a relationship yet he wants the physical embellishment that come with it. I rest my case, Tari."

At that point I was lost in translation. I didn't see the connection of literature or Olivia just had to throw it in there for aesthetics and phonetics. I tiptoed away. Children of today.

Chapter 20

Back in the village of Mara Valley, preparations were under way for the coming of the rain celebrations. I figured it would not be necessary to perform rain making ceremonies as even the small rivers were in overflow. My opinion did not matter in these important socio-economic matters. My jurisdiction ended in my yard concerning such matters. While I could discipline other kids in and around the village, issues of rain making were beyond me. They were for the select few, the chosen ones like Eti. I took pride in my capabilities and not once did I ever impose myself on anyone and I was not about to start. I knew my duties and responsibilities, and I carried them well. I remember one time at Sekuru Braki's funeral, it rained incessantly. No one seemed to mind the rain.

However, on the day of his burial, mourners mumbled about the rain been excessive and yearned for a bit of sunshine so the grave could be dug smoothly and the burial process would also proceed in a dry space. Mother's father had told us many times about how we could stop the rain when necessary. He shared various methods depending on the time of day it rained. If we woke up and it was still raining, early morning the first-born child, last-born, or an only child— who, by default, was both first and last born—had to go outside. He would then instruct the rain to stop by talking to it and throwing a short piece from the handmade traditional handheld broom *(kukanda kahuswa kemutsvairo)*. He had to do this before talking to anyone, making it essential to attempt this before dawn. Also, gender did not matter, both girls and boys could perform this trick. It was also popular on Christmas Day when we grew tired of the rain all week and wished to go out to the growth point for festivities. On such occasions, my eldest brother would do the honours, and twice it worked like magic. However, there was an instance when it failed. Mother explained that it was because he was angry. She could see his anger, and he later confessed that he was upset for not going to Salisbury with our father.

Whether rain stopping was morally right or not remained controversial. To this day, this issue continues to engender controversy. Nevertheless, I passed down this tradition to my children and younger relatives. Another method which grandfather had taught us was the one I applied at Sekuru Braki's funeral. I asked one of the older aunties for the deceased's shirt and she gave me without qualms as soon as I explained my odd request. It was a bizarre request as the dead are treated with dread and respect at the same time. She handed me a viscose shirt which I unbuttoned and hung in the middle of the wash line in the direction of the wind such that as the shirt flung about in the air, it dispersed the rain. It was the literal version of the nursery rhyme, *"rain rain go away, come again another day."* Within ten minutes, the sky cleared and the wind died down making room for a cool breeze. The rain stopped. All aunties ululated while Sekuru Braki's *sahwira* (best friend) pranced around the coffin, ululating and making gratitude utterances. The sisters-in-law then swept the pathway from the house leading to the gravesite, and all proceedings went as planned. I thanked myself as well as Sekuru Braki for heeding my call. This is where

Tarisai and I disagreed. At some point, she told me outright that that incident was a mere coincidence and otherwise, God answered the prayers of the many mourners who prayed for the rain to stop. Whereas mother said I had really stopped the rain. For the sake of sanity and peace, we all decided to let it end there. I am probably the only one who occasionally revisits that story when I feel belittled or just happy and frivolous, like on this day when I knew that rain making was out of my bounds. I found comfort in knowing my contribution was useful in other equally important areas of life.

Even Tarisai acknowledged my help in teaching her what she called "climatology". Even her Geography teacher and classmates were amazed at some of her precision. Tarisai knew how to interpret the winds and rain patterns. She observed the chickens' behaviour during the rainy season, especially that stretch from December to April when more rainfall watered the earth. Some of the tricks she learned were from me and others, but others were from general observations passed down from Mbuya Zvirevo and other respected elders. She knew that if the chickens came out to scratch and eat, the rain would likely persist overnight or throughout the day, with no end in sight. On the other hand, if the chickens went into hiding in their coop, that signalled the rain would be short-lived.

* * *

Mangondi's sudden eagerness in herding cattle was unsettling. Cattle herding was communal with families taking turns at the task. My husband said that Mangondi's household herded cattle more often than usual such that it sparked suspicion. No one could quite figure his intentions. A lot of women whispered about him on their way from the rivers, but they liked him describing how manly and active he was. Infatuation is often a disabler of sanity, worse when it shrivels into love, it can result in loss of character and purpose.

Mangondi learnt about the various pesticides and fungicides to protect herds and crops from infections. This earned him respect in the community. Moreso, because the locals held that wealth was in the land, hence any attack on plants and livestock was an enemy and Mangondi was the conqueror. Furthermore, in collaboration with Mara Cooperation for Land, Water and Wildlife, he went around the countryside educating fellow villagers about best practices in farming. It was thus imperative that he earned people's love and appreciation in spite of his shenanigans. Everyone who cared to know, knew how much he loathed his sister. Nevertheless, he fulfilled his obligations towards her as big brother and as the eldest in the family. Besides, an old saying goes, *"hukama haugezwe nesipo setsvina,"* (familial bonds can never be washed away with soap like dirt).

Over the past three weeks, Mangondi had taken on the role of mentoring young herd boys, supposedly to teach them proper grazing techniques. However, he harboured ulterior motives, which he discussed with his cronies under the rising sun's rays. Mangondi lived by the motto, 'Rise before the sun, and you'll have all your fears and desires under your rays.' It was widely known that his primary desire was success, achieved through any means necessary, even if it meant eliminating anyone in his path. Cunning and ambitious, Mangondi extended his influence beyond his immediate surroundings, teaching children in neighbouring villages of Mashangu and Mikoto.

A thief is always a step or two ahead, just as Mangondi was. Despite his shortcomings and unfounded hatred for his sister, he was widely liked by the general populace. Some revered him for his drumming skills and community empowerment efforts. If chieftaincy were determined by general election, he could easily win, having stolen the hearts of many, particularly women and young men who saw him as a role model. He epitomized masculinity and drumming excellence, his well-toned physique enhancing his appeal. Among his admirers, one secret admirer stood out, and he knew it. With his drum, he could easily cast a love spell if he put his mind to it, though he didn't care much about women, or so it was generally believed. He was married to one woman, yet his embrace was not limited to her alone. His status as a performer often led him to engage in friendly hugs with others, which were mostly innocent gestures of curiosity and joviality, devoid of any deeper meaning. Even men from the city hired him on their special occasions. Rumour had it that a renowned television broadcaster approached him to play the drum for news bulletin intros and interludes, but he declined, claiming he would never be a puppet of the white regime. He skilfully averted this topic, leaving it shrouded in speculation, and his default response to any unfavourable discussion was, "all rumour is humour, laugh it off." Perhaps that was also part of his charm, single-mindedness, and decisiveness no matter the circumstances. He was like a river, never changing course. To him, altering his path was akin to 'losing one's peoplehood,' as he put it.

The common courtesy dictated that people, especially children, look away when elders scratched their groin. Mangondi scratched, or appeared to scratch, at least three times in the afternoon when the kids were weary and inattentive. They even grew accustomed to this routine of looking away at least thrice or so. It seemed queer that none of them giggled, as kids were normally bound to do. Perhaps he cast a spell on them.

The teacher in him manifested whenever he saw multitudes, especially when he could view the tops of their heads and the listeners' eyes were lifted towards him as if waiting for manna. He started his training with anecdotes dotted with wit, keeping the kids engaged by asking practical everyday questions yet with complex applications. He taught well. When asked why he did not enrol in teacher training college, he joked that no school wanted dramas nor drummers.

The windy day marked the end of training. He made these closing remarks, "Little farmers, I will say it again and again. Never forget this single overarching life skill. After your Creator, fear your wife and this pesticide here," he lifted it for all to see. The kids rolled in laughter, while others whistled to show the highest form of excitement, and some even broke into short dances. While the kids frolicked, he scratched his crotch, as usual, getting his privacy.

However, in this instance, Mangondi poured about a cupful of pesticide into the dip tank. Every other day during training, he either poisoned the dip water while scratching or while playing pretend-hide and seek with the kids. He let out a trickle at a time for fear of overdose, but today he hit the final nail. Satisfied with himself, he dismissed the herd boys and went to update his crew of their apparent success. They were all convinced it was a foolproof plan and victory was certain. Only time delayed their celebration. Mangondi knew that using pesticides in any illegal or deliberately harmful manner, especially contaminating water sources for livestock, was unethical and posed serious risks to both animals and humans. It is important to use pesticides responsibly and in accordance with local regulations. The golden rule applies:

"when in doubt, leave it out." It is better to do nothing than try something that may endanger not only your life but others' too. Mangondi had a concoction of organophosphates, a class of insecticides that affect the nervous system of insects, along with pyrethroids, which are generally milder and considered less harmful to humans and animals. He also had herbicides, which he overused to contaminate the dip tank. Despite his moderation in poisoning the water, he still exposed both livestock and humans to potential adverse effects. His intention was to cause short-term harm with far-reaching consequences for his target.

A week after Mangondi's renowned training, havoc struck the village. Whether it was due to January disease or foot and mouth, no one really knew at that stage. The district administrators were puzzled, and the pressure from the villagers demanding plausible explanations and quick resolution to curb the problem only worsened the situation. Shocked administrators tried to pacify them with theoretical illustrations and frameworks, but they were not swayed. They remained adamant in their urgent and loud demand for tangible explanations, dismissing the theoretical explanations as hogwash textbook assumptions.

"That's the danger of school, see why I did not send my sons to school beyond Standard Three," one grey-haired man fumed.

"Indeed, it stops grown hairy men from using their brains. How dare he preach to us, "according to page fifty-five, do we eat pages, what's fifty-five compared to this legion of cattle," the men raved and ranted while exaggerating. There were not even a thousand cows in the region. Panic and despondency flooded the villages. Their livelihood and legacy lay in the livestock. The very cattle they so much cared for. Moreover, they paid bi-annual contributions towards pesticides and other fumigants. Indeed, an explanation was necessary. Mangondi owed the villagers a solid communique as he was one of the training facilitators under Mara Cooperation for Land, Water and Wildlife. The villagers, both men and women, clamoured for clarity, their voices echoing through the dusty roads of Mara like a chorus of uncertainty. They needed answers, unaware that not all answers are solutions and not all solutions are answers. One may find himself sleeping with the enemy.

Having little knowledge about cattle diseases, I found myself intrigued by the mystery of the disease afflicting our seemingly healthy livestock. Reflecting on missed opportunities, I lamented not taking Mr. Winston's optional lessons on animal husbandry. At the time, I misunderstood his intentions, fearing he aimed to teach us to treat our husbands like animals. My limited understanding and perhaps pride or ignorance evaded me. Though my husband may annoy me at times, I wouldn't want to degrade him to the level of an animal. I cherish him, flaws and all, just as he cherishes me. Now, as the veil of ignorance lifted, I recognised the wisdom in acquiring such knowledge, seeing its potential to illuminate the shadows of our current plight. Now, I wish I had that knowledge so I could contribute meaningfully instead of waiting for the rain to make myself useful. While cattle rearing may not be my forte, I possess expertise in other areas that I can leverage to contribute meaningfully. Of note is my beer making, a skill useful for events like the upcoming ritual ceremony at my mother's homestead.

Chapter 21

On the momentous day, Eti was in form and shape as she moved to the rhythms of traditional music in the yard. Her famous brother led the drummers as the rattlers embraced the charm of the drum with straight faces hiding their sophistication in subtle hints of mystery and half smiles. Rattling was also a parade of marriage readiness for any graceful and willing maiden just as drumming, singing, or jiving was. However, today Mangondi even forgot he had a wife, all his vile was wild unleashed. With each drumbeat, he moved one beat closer to victory.

After years serving as Pfumojena's spirit medium, Eti affectionately earned the nickname Mbuya Zvirevo. During her trances, she would often utter phrases like, "*ndine zvirevo newe*" (I have words for you), and her words were regarded as wise, akin to the wisdom found in Proverbs, which is translated in Shona to *Zvirevo*. Converted Christians and other villagers alike sought her counsel, drawn by her reputation for dispensing insightful wisdom, and many believed that her pronouncements had a prophetic quality, earning her the name Zvirevo. However, as a devout Christian, my daughter Tarisai struggled with the conflict between her faith and her grandmother's practices. She knew that consulting spirit mediums was explicitly forbidden in the Bible, and she grappled with the tension of honouring her grandmother while remaining faithful to her Christian beliefs. This turmoil cast a shadow over her relationship with Eti, as Tarisai wrestled with questions of loyalty and obedience to God's commandments, especially when her words were juxtaposed to the book of Proverbs. It was on days like today that she would be conflicted whether to support the ceremony or distance herself.

Singing formed an integral part of ceremony formalities, infusing the air with the vibrant rhythms of local songs. As the community gathered, voices rose in harmonious melodies, and feet moved in accented steps to the beat of drums. The rhythmic drumming of Mangondi echoed through the air, punctuating the lively atmosphere of the ceremony. Despite his skilled performance, there was a wry smile playing on his lips, hinting at a hidden agenda beneath the surface. "*Iyee he ha he*, (praise chants)" joyful chanters erupted in unison. Meanwhile Eti emerged from a circle of elders who had surrounded her in greeting. Some of them were several years older than her yet they bestowed reverent respect on her. They honoured the great ancestor upon her, who saw the sun before them all. Who walked the foothills of Mara and beyond before the year of the locusts. Even Chaminuka was younger than Pfumojena who rested upon Eti. Rumour said that Chaminuka was often in conversation with him which is perhaps why Eti's presence resonated with grandeur. She epitomised excellence. Chaminuka was a legendary spirit medium in his time, but Tarisai had other views.

Amidst the festive atmosphere, a cow was ceremoniously axed in one swift strike, a testament to the skilled hands of experienced individuals who ensured minimal trauma to the animal. The gathered crowd erupted into joyous ululations and continued singing, their voices blending with the rhythmic pounding of drums. However, Tarisai's attention was drawn to Mbuya Zvirevo, her grandmother, as she approached the fallen beast with solemn reverence.

In a striking display of spiritual connection, Mbuya Zvirevo, adorned in ceremonial regalia, approached the fallen beast with solemn respect, her steps measured and purposeful. The majestic animal lay before her, its lifeblood already spilled in the name of tradition. With a gentle hand, she reached out to touch the fallen beast in its still form, a silent acknowledgment of the sacrifice made.

As she knelt beside the cow, the crowd watched their eyes fixed on her every movement. With practiced precision, Mbuya Zvirevo leaned forward, her lips meeting the wound where the axe had struck. She drank deeply, the taste of blood a tangible connection to the spirits of the ancestors. What Eti was drinking was called *muropa* which literally translates to "in blood" and I explained to Tarisai that it was different to the blood meal (*musiya*) which was blood cooked after slaughter and consumed hot by select people. This *muropa* was essential for the spirit mediums. Drinking raw from the cow.

Beside Eti, another spirit medium approached, his demeanour respectful as he joined in the ritual, albeit with a smaller sip, acknowledging the sanctity of the moment. Shortly afterwards, Mbuya Zvirevo continued to drink, her unwavering commitment to tradition evident in every sip. Together, they had honoured the fallen cow, each sip a solemn tribute to the traditions that bound them together. All the while, the rhythmic beat of drums echoed through the air, underscoring the sacredness of the moment.

Observing the scene, Tarisai's brow furrowed as she couldn't help but express concern for the welfare of animals.

Turning to her father, she voiced her worries, "But isn't this... I mean, isn't it too much for the cow?"

Her father, my husband, a pillar of the community, reassured her with a gentle smile, "I understand your concerns, Tari my child. But rest assured, the cow was slaughtered with utmost care by experienced hands. It's a tradition deeply rooted in our culture, and while I once thought of reporting it to the SPCA myself, I've come to understand its importance for our community's social welfare."

He continued, "Moreover, the cow doesn't suffer much. The skilled hands of our experienced men ensure that it dies instantly, without trauma."

Observing Tarisai, I couldn't help but sense the weight of her Christian faith, a calling to ministry that added another layer to her internal struggle. She nodded, her expression a mix of uncertainty and contemplation as she watched the ceremony unfold before her. She grappled with the complexities of tradition and modernity, the conflict evident in the furrow of her brow and the subtle shift of her gaze.

Some onlookers started calling out Eti, while others shouted Mbuya Zvirevo. Others chanted, "Thank you Pfumojena, we acknowledge you Mhazi," as the atmosphere filled with a sense of respect and gratitude. Eti staggered three steps and cringed, clutching her stomach as she made a U-turn, still hobbling. Her head remained bowed, weighed down by the weight of the moment, her discomfort palpable though the cause remained unknown. Her new aide, Miriam, rushed to her with an outstretched arm but she gestured her to stop with her listless left hand. By now, most of those present knew Mbuya Zvirevo enough to understand what either left or right meant in her world. They were familiar with her use of hands and the meaning attached.

Mbuya Zvirevo raised herself and attempted a few more laboured steps and she fell prostate on the hard earth. Raising her left hand was a bad omen in itself to those who were accustomed to her gestures. Spectators, from beyond Mara Valley gasped in disbelief as to why no one rushed to revive her at least. Thanks to Mr. Winston, my knowledge of first aid indicated that at this point she needed to be placed in the recovery position. But knowing my mother, once she told you to back off, you had to comply. It broke my heart to see her helpless like that. Mighty Eti, etched on a collapsing hilltop with no harness, seemed to freefall at the speed of light. Well, that is what it felt like watching her struggle to rise up. It was agonising. What made me more scared was that left hand she raised. Despite all that, I had a small level of peace in my heart. My heart skipped a beat when she collapsed, but then it settled. Whatever damage was happening, I believed it would pass without losing Mbuya Zvirevo. I am sure Miriam felt the same. One glance at her gave me the reassurance I needed. Even though she was my mother, Mbuya Zvirevo was better known to Miriam than to any of us at home. Tarisai knew her in certain aspects, but Miriam spent her time understanding her, not only learning from her but also learning about her. Miriam had dropped out of school to follow mother, but I protested and sent her back to school. She was my brother's child, and he was unperturbed by her drastic decision to leave secondary school. I wouldn't have it. Infuriated, I fought with my mother, angry at how she could even allow that, but all she said was that it was Miriam's destiny. Fate. I sent Miriam back to school, and that was it. No one contested. I was prepared to report to the education district offices for violation. After days of exchanging words and failed negotiations, they finally gave in. The compromise was that Miriam would at least attend school until she reached eighteen years of age, then she could make an independent choice. I wondered if it was the food that made them agree to her foolish idea. Religion and food can be the enemies of humanity. Religion is the opium of the people, blinding them to reason and nourishing them with false promises. Yet, it's often the very sustenance they cling to, unwilling to question its effects on their minds and society. That's why some people said it is better to drink beer than concern yourself with many doctrines, though that was a dangerous sentiment.

As the community gathered around Mbuya Zvirevo, concern etched on their faces, a group of women quickly mobilized to carry her back to her hut. Despite her weakened state, there was a glimmer of hope in their eyes as they worked together to ease her pain. They mumbled and whispered that this was the first time such a thing had occurred during this precious ceremony. Still, no one had answers.

Inside her humble dwelling, the atmosphere was tense as Miriam, with a newfound determination, took charge of caring for Mbuya Zvirevo. With a steady hand and a heart full of love, she administered the medicinal herbs prescribed by the traditional healer. However, the herbs proved to be potent, causing Mbuya Zvirevo to vomit and experience diarrhoea. Mbuya Zvirevo's other brother Ngondo, who worked as a nurse aide at Mara District Clinic, had rushed there, and the resident doctor prescribed an oral rehydration solution and medication to cleanse her system and aid her liver detoxification. Despite objections from some traditional healers, these treatments were administered alongside traditional medicines. Tarisai declared healing for her grandmother, praying for her at her bedside, mumbling inaudible words. Mbuya Zvirevo's recovery was from a combination of faith, herbs and lab tested medicine, not sure which of the three dominated. If I had added another aspect, time, Tarisai would have objected saying the One who controls time healed her. Sometimes I played around with her just to test her firmness in her beliefs.

Meanwhile, Mangondi and his allies watched from the sidelines, their expressions betraying their true feelings of satisfaction. They had been waiting for an opportunity like this, and now that Mbuya Zvirevo was incapacitated, they made a candid victory dance.

As the days passed, Miriam's diligent care and the healing properties of the medicine began to take effect, alongside prayers from well-wishers. I, too, prayed for my mother. Mbuya Zvirevo's strength slowly returned, and with each passing day, she grew stronger despite her lack of appetite for solid food.

It was a testament to the resilience of the human spirit and the power of love and determination. Miriam's unwavering commitment to her grandmother's well-being played a crucial role in her recovery, proving that sometimes, it takes a village to heal a soul.

Tarisai shared these Bible verses with Eti during her recovery period. "I do not understand what I do. For what I want to do I do not do, but what I hate I do. And if I do what I do not want to do, I agree that the law is good. As it is, it is no longer I myself who do it, but it is sin living in me." I asked her to explain as I doubted those were meant to make her feel better. She answered to me that in the fullness of time, she would understand, and so would I understand why I shared those verses.

Chapter 22

After Eti fell sick, she was instructed by her Pfumo-jena to head to a distant village called Mukumbura, towards the Zimbabwe, Mozambique border post. It had to be dome for reason us mere ordinary people would not understand. Only those who see beyond time could understand. Well, Tarisai accompanied me to visit her. She was on her college holiday. The ride by bus was close to 12 hours; it was tiring just sitting on the bus, let alone driving it across hilly terrain. I felt pity for the driver. We had boarded at Mbare Musika bus station at 3am only to arrive when the owls were howling.

Glaring into the distance, a flickering light could be spotted about half a mile away. Into the darkness, we began shuffling our dusty feet towards that light. In an instant, my hair stood on end.

Danger! Danger!

As if in a flashback, I recalled the bidding heed of the driver whose bus we had just disembarked. He had vehemently warned us to proceed to the last stop and walk back to our intended bus stop at dawn, "No one treads these lonely roads after twilight," he looked oblivious, sighed and continued, "It is their time, better not disturb them," with that, he shuddered.

"Who are they?" Tarisai demanded. "If no one on this bus will respond, fine, we will stop where we want. There's nothing on earth that I can't confront, even under the earth. Let them, whoever they are, face me!" she said in a heavy overtone. The rest of the passengers shrugged, while others clutched their temples. Deep inside, I hoped Tarisai was jesting and that we wouldn't drop off in the thick of the night. To my horror and shock, she shouted, "Matenga!"

That signalled the driver to stop at the ill-fated bus stop. As I shuffled along the narrow passage, I could feel anxious eyes staring at us. Even then, my heart made a thud and I knew that this was a bad decision. Tarisai young as she was, was not someone you could convince otherwise once her mind was made up. Being 21 had flared up her confidence in both her calling and purpose in life. Even her stubbornness mushroomed. "What a nuisance she is," I murmured.

"Did you say something?"

"Ahh, yes, yes I said it's cold."

As my hair stood, I remembered all the eerie stories we had shared, chuckling about how people can be stupid, coming up with such fake stories. Now! This was reality. Immediately I heard voices moving in the wind and the sound of feet scurrying. The sound grew louder within seconds and a distinct voice resonated, "That's her!"

I went numb. All this while Tarisai remained stoic, being the brave young woman she was.

"What do you want, we don't know you? If you are looking for trouble I am here!" she resounded fiercely. Clearly, she wasn't scared; she remained unperturbed. Such confidence, such bravery. Everything became still, even time stopped. All was silent. Footsteps could be heard retreating further into a bush, far from us.

It was soon after sunrise that I asked how we had gotten here. We were in a hut. I had a hazy recollection of that. Tarisai sneered menacingly, and I was frightened. Knowing her, I knew such a laugh signified a nasty prank. My mind softened a bit when the sneer turned into a guffaw. Infectiously, I joined the laughter. I had no idea though why we were laughing so hard.

"Oh, you don't know, did you think you slept on the bus?" Tarisai teased, nudging my elbow and bringing me off balance. I fell onto my back onto the rugged sleeping mat. For some reason, I felt at peace despite having so many questions about the previous night. Soon, I heard my mother's reassuring voice greeting me. She recalled to me how we had arrived and what we had heard in the night. She praised Tarisai for her bravery and strength in her faith. That is the day I became a real Christian. I was ready to ditch my scepticism about it. I asked Tarisai to help me understand more. She even told me about how Peter's shadow from the Bible could heal people as he passed. She explained to me that, it was a matter of choice, not force, to believe in her God. Anyway, the purpose of our trip was to take mother back home. Tarisai claimed in her prayers, there was a revelation to bring her grandmother back home. I believed her. Maybe I just missed my mum. Also, that time father was in Kindu and rumour spread that Emma was occasionally going to help him with his laundry. That infuriated me. I knew my mother would just brush it off for the sake of preserving her marriage but not under my watch. I had an argument with father and the whole mining compound gathered. I made such a scene his boss gave him a pay raise so he was promoted from the compound to the foreman's quarters to cover his humiliation. I did not trust that Emma at all. She had always been jealous of Eti since their maiden days. My father Sansirai was a hunk in his days. He also had the manners. So, I caused havoc and that inspired me to also agree with Tarisai to bring Eti closer to her man.

* * *

Tarisai had heard numerous stories about people who vanished in so-called sacred places, especially in Mukumbura. It is one thing to believe in superstition, but it is another to live in the supernatural. Perhaps she had acted in haste and let her anger get the better of her, instead of calming down and wandering away. This was her first time overreacting to such an extent. Mother's neighbour in Mukumbura had shouted at her for praying and teaching me about Jesus. What angered her the most was when he poured some "cleansing water" on her and blown snuff to her face. Her own grandmother never did that; they co-existed in their differences out of mutual respect. Generally, she was a level-headed, phlegmatic person who knew how to tolerate and endure the most harrowing and gruelling discomforts of life. At one time, she stayed with Uncle Mike and his wife, and she complained that she felt suffocated. Uncle Mike's wife, Sanelisiwe, though an amicable lady, was an irritating, conceited woman who got in people's way by manipulation. She exaggerated her amiability, which was evident to everyone, including her husband and other relatives. They laughed each time she over-welcomed or over-pampered someone. She also mastered the game of annoyance and self-centeredness so well that she played her cards five times ahead. Those new to her gimmicks felt loved and appreciated, when in fact, all she cared about was herself. Uncle Mike didn't divorce her for the sake of their kids and because he subscribed to the notion of "better the devil you know than the angel you don't. Over time, most relatives countered her fake love by playing their cards ten times ahead of her five steps. Her personality was a mere display of feigned, superficial affection and care, which was fleeting like dew in December. Though unaware herself, she proved to many a valuable lesson of the hollowness of false gentility. Those who genuinely liked her after that discovery were few. The rest merely accommodated for the sake of their familial relations; otherwise, she was a nuisance to put up with. A noisy mosquito in the dead of a sweltering hot October night, disturbing an exhausted sleeper. At the first slap, that mosquito is gone. That's how those around her viewed her, except for those few from her own family whom she liked. Tarisai had a thick skin and mastered the art of braving her annoying aunt's shenanigans. Sincerity was important to her, so being in this forest was an act she had made out of serious agitation, stretched beyond her limits.

Tarisai found herself surrounded by peculiar trees, each bearing identical scars and bruises. They resembled old men with mouths agape, their wrinkled features conveying either pain or shock—it was difficult to discern the exact emotion. What was unmistakable, however, was that these were no ordinary trees.

Similar phenomena occurred near the burning mountain in Chiringe. At dusk, distant trees on Chiringe mountain would ignite, filling the sky with smoke. Throughout the night, the fire blazed, yet it posed no threat to the villages below. Legend had it that if one rose early enough before the elephants' bathing time, they might witness the fire dwindling, revealing a line of men and women wandering near the embers as if searching for something. This myth persisted even as far as Mara, though I never personally witnessed the mountain ablaze.

"Do you feel the same way I do right now?" she asked, her voice quavering and her eyebrows arched upwards. As if by instinct, she flung her arms wide open to shield the little boy she had joined along her way at the entrance of the forest. She turned to look at him, gesturing with her hand that she was waiting for a reply—an answer that never came.

"Well, you know we cannot really say much in here, right?" That moment, her hair stood on end and she froze. She was alone.

In the Inyangani mountains of the far east, where beautiful scenery adorns the peaks, lurk ominous sacred tales beneath the canopy of lush greenery. In the 80s, there were official reports of children who disappeared in those mountains. Despite extensive searches, no trace of them has ever been found. Here Tarisai stood, having walked with a boy who wasn't truly a boy. He was there, yet not there—a spectral presence. It is said that in these sacred mountains, speaking aloud may anger the spirits of the land, leading to various consequences. Some may become lost for a while, others may faint, find themselves outside the forest, or worse, vanish forever. Tarisai stood there in momentary confusion, grappling with the weight of the ancient tales.

* * *

A lanky man with a sideways swagger and a bagful of dreadlocks asked for directions at dusk. He was directed to the chief's homestead as per custom. He sought help all the way from Slobela, he had travelled to Mukumbura but he got a rotten donkey. He told the chief he believed this was his last stop.

"I had a dream," he narrated to the chief whose eyes bulged with each sentence he uttered.

With a soft stamp of his knobkerrie, the chief summoned his right-hand man, a hefty figure bearing scars from battles with crocodiles, wielding an axe. After the chief whispered to him, the man brought water in a broken gourd. This act was more than a mere offering—it was the ultimate test, a tradition passed down through generations of chiefs. If he was lying, he would fail this sacred rite. "Many a time, we have welcomed thieves, witches, and nuisances under the guise of genuine need. Do I see that in you?" The chief's voice carried a weight of scrutiny.

"The genteel people of my village have entertained gringos, thinking they are good people. Do I sense that in you?" His gaze pierced through any facade.

"We have sat around the fire for dinner with lions in sheep's skin, assuming they are lambs. Are you a lamb or a lion?" The question hung heavy in the air, demanding an honest answer.

The chief eyed and weighed him from toe to head and back again. "This water has crocodile bile. If you are a lion, you will be food for the vultures in no time. But if you are indeed a lamb, you will graze with others tomorrow.

Choose wisely. You have a free passage if you decide now. Are you drinking, or are you leaving?" With that, the chief spat a bluish phlegm, the final testament to the gravity of the moment.

The man wrung his hands nervously, biting his lip. He scratched his head as if searching for answers amidst the tangled thoughts. His gaze lingered on the chief's phlegm, now spread in a small mound near his bag.

Meanwhile, the beefy man stared into the distant hills, lost in contemplation amid the swirling dust of passing gusts. It was said that a yard swept at dusk would reveal the footprints of witches if they happened to pass that way. Those who witnessed such footprints would chant spells to reverse any enchantments or ill incantations spoken.

The weight of the chief's question hung heavy in the air, and the man knew his decision would determine his fate. and amidst the dust of some girls sweeping nearby. It was said if a yard was swept and dusk will leave footprints of witches if they pass that way. All they would do is take that footprint and chant spells to reverse whatever enchantments and ill incantations were spoken.

The visitor bowed his head, as if in prayer, then raised it again, determination etched in his expression. He glared into the cup containing the bile, swallowing hard as his Adam's apple protruded almost double. Beads of sweat formed on the crest of his forehead, and a few drops of runny mucus splashed onto the dusty ground. Closing his eyes, he brought the cup near his torso, as if weighing his decision. With a deep sigh, he raised the cup to his nose, recoiling at the re-pulsive odour with subtle hints of something sinister. His stomach churned, and he hesitated.

Squelching back a wave of nausea, he opened his eyes, as if bidding farewell to the world. Slowly, he turned his head to the left, lowering the cup to his dry lips while he gritted his teeth. Sweat formed on his eyebrows. Noticing his reluc-tance, the chief yelled at him to take a gulp. And in that moment, as he obliged, his body shuddered, consumed by the consequences of his choice.

* * *

Tarisai stormed into the chiefs courtyard as she ran with her slippers clutched in one armpit. Panting and grasping for breath she pointed to the direction of the Chiringe Moun-tains. She bent holding her knees while coughing towards the ground. How se ran that fast was a mystery. The chief gestured his advisor to get her some water and someone ushered her to sit down.

A smile lurched on the visitor's face followed by a heavy sigh. He looked to the heavens as if thanking them even though it could be a brief delay of his fate. He listened intently as Tarisai narrated answering the chiefs questions. He pinched the soil for good luck, whether it was fact or fable that it worked, he would soon find out.

Eti emerged from her hut just as Tarisai finished relaying her ordeal in the sacred mountain. She saw the stranger who was trembling. The chief's advisor was a wise man who was renowned for his fast thinking. He whispered to the chief for a few minutes then the chief spoke. He cleared his throat and took a sip of water. He then poured some water on the ground and due to the terrain, the water flowed towards both Eti and Tarisai who were on seated opposite sides to the chief.

"Young man, thank your ancestors. These two females here confirm that you must be set free. Their sudden simultaneous appearance is a first in these lands. This procedure has never been disrupted before. Therefore, I set you free. You can sleep one night here and be on your way at dawn. That young man will show you were to sleep, after giving you food." The chief then poured more water on the ground.

The man expressed his heartfelt gratitude to the chief and to Eti and Tarisai. He lay prostate on the ground before the chief as he thanked him. The court was then dismissed. The man had a brief chat with Eti and Tarisai and other men who gathered to know more about him.

Tarisai only managed to say to the relieved dreadlocked man, "God loves everyone intimately and to the core. The wisdom is in the interpretation."

Chapter 23

The district council called for a meeting to address the issue plaguing our livestock. Apparently, they had conducted further investigation and consultation with the town council and the provincial agriculture board, not forgetting the traditional chiefs. The committee leading the meeting informed us that if cattle consume water contaminated with pesticides, various health issues may arise. In cattle, symptoms may include digestive problems, weight loss, and even reproductive issues. Additionally, the presence of pesticides in the bloodstream can potentially transfer into milk and meat. For humans consuming milk from cattle exposed to pesticides, there is a risk of absorbing these harmful substances into the bloodstream. Pesticides in milk can have adverse effects on human health, including potential impacts on the nervous and reproductive systems. Eating meat from such cattle may also pose health risks due to the accumulation of pesticides in the animal's tissues. This was all complex for me but my husband made it clearer. He said it was like drinking beer from poisoned rapoko.

The nearest vet from Kindu, after examining the sick cattle, suspected pesticide poisoning and advised the farmers to investigate the water source.

A farm owner burst in an uproar, "We trusted him for years, and he repays us like this? Our cattle are sick, and people in the community are suffering. He should have stuck to drumming and charming our women."

Zivai almost sobbing but holding back said, "My child drank that milk! What are the long-term consequences? Is he going to be, okay?"

The senior veterinarian replied in an empathetic voice, "We're doing our best to treat the cattle, but the effects of pesticide poisoning can be severe. As for the people, it depends on the concentration and duration of exposure. I recommend thorough medical check-ups which are being done in a makeshift mobile clinic organised by the provincial office. The chief's chairwoman will share more details about that."

All farmers and the rest of the villagers agreed in unison, "We can't let this happen again. We need to secure our water sources and ensure the safety of our products."

Eti who had watched the progression of the case in silence finally spoke, "I can't believe my own brother would do this to our family and the entire community. No doubt he hates me, but this!"

I nodded. "This wasn't just about poisoning cattle; it was a vendetta. How do we trust each other after something like this? I don't think I want to dance to his drums again. This is sickening."

The sympathetic and spectacled veterinarian added, "The personal motives make it even more complex. We must focus on healing the community, both physically and emotionally. Animals depend on us to care for them. This is unfair. I am hurt, " he said, his voice heavy with emotion. He took off his glasses and wiped his eyes while shaking his head. "I love animals. That's not just my job; it's my duty, my passion. No animal deserves this, especially to settle personal human scores.

The headman spoke with permission from the chief in absentia. "We need to rebuild trust and support one another. Family disputes should never jeopardise the well-being of our community. Legal actions against Mangondi will proceed, and we'll work on community-building initiatives to foster unity and resilience. He has to pay for his heinous crimes to the chief, to Eti and to the affected owners whose cattle drank from that dip tank. He should also serve jail term at Ndaitei Prison." Ululations and clapping filled the air, accompanied by murmuring and whispering. His wife, however, gave the loudest sneer. Well, what happens behind closed doors between husband and wife can be shocking. Not all marriages are rosy. She even clapped the hardest. She was even heard mumbling that he had finally got a taste of his own medicine. Well, it was now clear she was only staying with him for the sake of the children's welfare, to ensure they were raised in a unified household.

Mangondi was ushered into the room by the chief's security team. Eti seethed with anger. "How could you do this, Mangondi? Myself, our livelihood, the entire community is suffering because of your actions!"

He whistled showing no ounce of remorse, "You think it's that simple? You've always had everything handed to you, and I wanted to show everyone that you're not invincible. Eti, Eti, Mbuya Zvirevo, you have at all. I am the first son. I was the apple of my parents' eyes for ten years with no other sibling. I was their all. I was their precious gift form the ancestors. Then these other brothers of mine came, no problem. Then you, for whatever reason? Then the ancestors chose you yet it was me all this time holding this happy family together. My birth brought relief and joy to our parents after they struggled to conceive for a whole year and you know who the leaders and village mongers pointed fingers at them for delaying conception. Was it their fault , they tried. And I became a light to them. Do you know why I play the drum so well, so I can beat it so loud that I don't hear your name mentioned. And, here we are, you should have revoked that calling and focused on basketweaving." With that he bit his lower lip and sulked bowing his head.

Eti chuckled and shook her head three times starting from the right. Then her smile vanished. "This isn't about me, first son. It's about the community, about innocent people and animals suffering because of your selfish vendetta. You should have poisoned my tea or food like you have tried to do in the past. Why drag innocent people into your fight? How could the ancestors have chosen you even if they wanted, with such vile thoughts you have displayed over the years"

"You don't understand the pressure I've been under. I needed them to see you as flawed, to level the playing field."

"There are better ways to deal with family issues! You've not only hurt me but everyone who trusted us. What were you thinking?"

Mangondi now seemingly teary, "I didn't think it would get this far. I just wanted to make a point. I am sorry Mother of Cheukai."

"Well, you've made your point, brother. Now we have to pick up the pieces. You're not just my brother anymore; you're someone who put our entire community at risk." The rest of the spectators gasped and sighed as they followed the conversation. They each left shuffling to their houses and shaking their heads.

Despite the confrontation, Mangondi, fuelled by resentment, hatched a new plan to further undermine his sister. He discreetly spread rumours about Mbuya Zvirevo's involvement in the poisoning, creating doubt and division among the townspeople, once again. The same way he did when Zivai's baby was stolen. Mangondi also talks about how Mbuya Zvirevo saved the strange man with the dreadlocks, saying she was ever cunning from the start. Together with her granddaughter Tarisai, they had allegedly fooled the village and freed that spy, claimed Mangondi. He further argued why Mbuya Zvirevo had taken the side of Christianity in freeing the man. He claimed she was using Tarisai as a front to cause contention in the village.

The community, already shaken by the previous events, became suspicious and started questioning her integrity. However, most people were on her side. Those who were against her, such as Uncle Zano and his close family excluding his wife, loathed her with a passion. Eti was aware of these shenanigans by means of the spirit of Pfumojena upon her, yet she seemed to ignore the plot. She faced increasing isolation and hostility from Mangondi's cronies. They stopped her from attending their ceremonies and meetings. For the sake of peace, the headman advised Mbuya Zvirevo to lay low and avid public appearances. He also warned that Tarisai should stay in the township until the air was clear.

As tensions escalated, the truth began to unravel, exposing the Mangondi's deceptive web and the extent of his vendetta. The village, realising they had been manipulated once again, turned against Mangondi demanding accountability for his actions.

Eti, having weathered another storm, emerged stronger, supported by those of us who through Mangondi's schemes. I let Tarisai visit the village and she was happy to be reunited to her grandma. What made her happier was when Eti informed her that she was retiring from her role and would relinquish being a spirit medium once due process was conducted in the traditional way under the spiritual leadership of her clan. Eti also explained that this transition did not transfer anything to Mangondi. "The ancestors would know the best course of action," she concluded.

Chapter 24

As I gazed into the mirror, the meaning of my name echoed in my mind. "Look back," it whispered, prompting me to revisit the chapters of my life. Each reflection held a story, woven with moments of joy, trials, and growth. In the tapestry of memories, I found the threads that shaped me into the person staring back. As I embraced the journey, the mirror became a portal to self-discovery, revealing the intricate beauty of my past and the promising horizon of my future.

My ramblings, like a meandering river, flowed through the landscape of my memories, carving intricate channels, and revealing the hidden contours of my past. Each tangent became a tributary, contributing to the complex delta of my experiences. Like a curious traveler navigating through the labyrinth of recollections, I wandered among the ruins of forgotten moments and stumbled upon the blooming gardens of cherished memories. My ramblings, akin to the flight of a butterfly, danced from one petal of nostalgia to another, pollinating the landscape of my character with the essence of each encounter.

And so, as I conclude these ramblings, I find solace in the realisation that my name is not merely a linguistic label; it's a guiding light, urging me to revisit, learn, and grow. In the gallery of my reflections, I discover the masterpiece of a life transformed by grace, woven with threads of redemption, joy, and divine connection. The journey continues, and with each step forward, I carry the wisdom of looking back, guided by the teachings of Christ. Though torn between honoring the traditions of my past as a beer maker and dancer, and embracing the calling of my daughter, a devout Christian, I find strength in surrendering to the path illuminated by faith.

Amidst the indifference of my husband, I anchor my soul in unwavering love, finding peace in the knowledge that my steps are guided by a higher purpose. My husband's name, meaning, "What do we know?" reflects his easygoing nature, often drifting where the wind takes him, and sometimes appearing indecisive. Despite my initial reservations, he has proven to be a good husband. However, others have misconstrued his actions, branding him a puppet after his baptism, or a sellout for his extensive association with white farmers.

His unwavering support for my daughters, even at the expense of our relationship, often left me silently chastising him. Naive and prone to saying 'yes' to their requests, he annoyed me at times. However, when questioned about why we didn't have a son, his simple response, "Leave me alone," filled me with a sense of pride. He stood firm in his belief that children, regardless of gender, deserved equal attention and care.

During challenging times, such as when our daughter Tari incorporated Euler into every aspect of daily living, for once he stood by me, offering support and encouragement. Yet all this time, despite my efforts to steer Tari towards a more conventional path, he nurtured her dreams, insisting she had a calling from the Holy Spirit.

Though disappointed when he finally agreed to take Tari to Njanja for her leopard story, I rejoiced at the outcome. We had finally put the leopard cub story to rest. Despite our differences and misunderstandings, my love for him has only deepened over the years. And yes, there were times when I sulked—life with him was never short of surprises!

Tarisai's name means look. She is a Christian. Her name "look" serves as a constant reminder to delve into the depths of her being. Raised amidst the rich tapestry of her family's traditions and the steadfast teachings of Christianity, she grapples with a profound inner conflict.

On one hand, there's the ancient wisdom of her grandmother, a revered spirit medium whose rituals echo through generations. On the other, there's the comforting embrace of her Christian faith, with its promise of salvation and grace. Caught between these two worlds, Tarisai embarks on a journey of introspection. As she navigates the maze of conflicting beliefs and cultural heritage, Tarisai learns to trust her inner voice. And as she looks inward, she finds not just answers, but the strength to embrace her beliefs.

Eti, Mbuya Zvirevo, a revered figure in their community, holds a name shrouded in mystery. Derived from a dream of her great-grandfather, its meaning remains a secret, known only to the ancestors. Yet, her wisdom is undeniable. As a spirit medium, she serves as a bridge between the living and the spirit world. Her guidance is sought after, her insights revered. Also known by a nickname derived from speaking proverbial language, she is a depot of knowledge.

For all of us, it's a journey of discovery, navigating the delicate balance between faith and tradition, as we all seek to understand our own place within the enigmatic tapestry called family. However, I have something that still troubles me. I should have listened Tarisai, maybe my mother's poisoning could have been avoided.

Four weeks before the poisoning, Tarisai insisted on seeing her grandmother. No doubt she inherited stubbornness from me, but it bordered on defiance and obstinance. She pestered until you ended up thinking she was a pest. Her nickname 'Mosquito' arose because she could be a nuisance like Aunt Sanelisiwe. She denied being a nuisance; instead, she claimed the nickname came from being skinny like a mosquito. She had the same line, "A dragonfly is an apt fit, but if you suppose I am straight and skinny, I am a mosquito then. What can a simple girl do?" She chuckled, shrugging her shoulders.

Our response remained the same. "We are not saying you are a doorframe princess; you are just a nuisance, honey." We always laughed. That's what I liked about Tarisai. She had a sanguine temperament. It took an effort to upset her, except when it came to her faith.

Tarisai explained her recurring vision involving Mbuya Zvirevo. In her premonition, she described seeing scattered cattle in the fields, each carcass adorned with a bucket, while Mbuya Zvirevo stood with her back to them, as if leading them in a procession. According to Tarisai, this vision was ominous because her grandmother wore a white frock instead of her usual black skirt, indicating a transition into the afterlife. Tarisai insisted she needed to warn her grandmother. "Your father hasn't been paid for a while and you are studying. In short, it will be wasteful to spend money just to deliver that one message—"

"But Mum, don't you love your mother?" Tarisai said, her eyes pleading as she looked at me.

"You can't blackmail me. I'm older than you. We do love your granny, but circumstances are against us at the moment. We'll warn her when we see her at our next planned visit."

That was the moment I sealed my mother's fate. I should have listened to my daughter; we could have avoided this catastrophe. If she had died, I would struggle to forgive myself.

Chapter 25

The right path for me, Cheukai, is a journey of balance—a delicate intertwining of heritage and personal beliefs. I strive to honour the ancestral spirituality passed down by my mother, Mbuya Zvirevo, while embracing the fervent faith of my daughter, Tarisai.

I find strength in diversity, recognising that the tapestry of our family is woven with threads of different beliefs. It's not about choosing one path over the other but learning to harmonise the distinct melodies that shape our lives for the sake of peace and preservation of the family unit. Respect. Love. Tolerance.

I navigate this intricate dance, respecting the spirits my mother communes with and embracing the Christian faith that comforts my daughter. The right path, for me, is the one that fosters unity, understanding, and love within our family.

In the end, the right path is a personalised melody, a unique composition that resonates with the essence of who I am— a bridge between the worlds that shape our family's history.

My daughter's anger is a storm that occasionally sweeps through our harmonious existence. Her staunch Christian beliefs clash with the spiritual traditions of our family, creating thunderous moments of discord.

In those moments, I become a mediator, trying to calm the tempest within our home. It's a delicate dance, acknowledging her feelings while reaffirming the importance of embracing diversity in our spiritual journey. I understand that her anger is a product of passion for her beliefs. My role is to guide her toward a more tranquil understanding, fostering a space where love can outweigh the storms of disagreement. Yet, I remain steadfast in my commitment to harmony. It's crucial for her to see that our family's strength lies not in the absence of disagreements but in our ability to weather the storms together.

As I continue on this path of balance, I hope that the winds of understanding will eventually calm the storms, revealing a clearer, more tranquil horizon for our family. In the narrative of our family, the heroines emerge with distinct tales woven into the fabric of our history—my mother, Eti, the spirit medium whose connection to the unseen shaped our legacy.

Then there's my daughter, a beacon of strength in her unwavering Christian faith, navigating the complexities of our family's spiritual tapestry with resilience.

As for me, I find my heroism in being the bridge between generations and beliefs, seeking harmony amidst the clashes, and nurturing the unity that defines our family's resilience.

Together, we are the heroines of our own stories—each contributing a unique melody to the grand composition of our family's journey. It's in our diversity, our conflicts, and our shared moments of understanding that the true strength of our family lies.

In this intricate dance of spirituality, love, and acceptance, we navigate the chapters of our lives, creating a story that transcends individual narratives—a story of resilience, growth, and the enduring power of familial bonds.

In the symphony of our family, my husband was a rhythm I once deemed orchestrated by external forces—a puppet dancing to the whims of life's discordant melodies. Over time, I began to discern the subtle nuances in his dance—a dance not dictated by strings but guided by a desire for balance, a delicate choreography of responsibilities and aspirations. I grew to respect him as a maestro of his own fate, conducting the rhythms of his life with intentionality. His choices, once seen as mere reactions, revealed themselves as steps towards equilibrium. His need for balance became a harmonious echo, complementing my own journey of finding stability within our family's complex dynamics. In understanding him, I discovered a shared pursuit of harmony. In acknowledging his agency, I found a partner not confined by strings but empowered by the freedom to choose his steps—a dance partner in the intricate ballet of our shared life. Though he may have been renamed John at baptism, he remained the unassuming Tazivei I married many moons ago. I couldn't help but notice that he seemed to enjoy hugging me quite frequently. I couldn't decide if this was some new lesson from his baptism classes or just his unique way of marking his territory.

In the intricate composition of our family's story, my husband emerged as a key contributor—a melody intertwining with mine, creating a duet that resonates with the beauty of balance.

My other daughter, Zivai, the carefree spirit of our family, dances through life with an infectious joy, finding solace in the traditions that anchor our roots. Her laughter, like a melodic refrain, echoes through our home, intertwining with the spiritual hymns and rhythmic beats that define our family's unique composition. Although still widowed, she continues to embrace tradition, weaving her own narrative into the fabric of our family's history—a new melody harmonising with the echoes of the past. It is my wish that she marries again, someone her age, a companion. I've heard that one of the foremen at Kindu, a cultured and well-mannered senior bachelor, has been showing interest in her. However, most villagers and his colleagues believe he's been unlucky in finding a wife due to rumours of a curse or bad luck surrounding him. I wonder how Zivai is responding to his advances. All I want is for her to experience the warmth of a happy home once more.

Years ago, I refused when they wanted her loafer brother-in-law to inherit her. As a mother, I stood at the crossroads of tradition and personal convictions, grappling with the weight of familial expectations. The decision to allow such an arrangement would not be an easy one, for it carried implications that would extend beyond her immediate grief. It would torment her and ruin her future. That custom of imposing husbands on young widows had to stop. It was ruthless. My heart ached for my daughter, and in that difficult moment, I navigated the fine line between honouring tradition and safeguarding her autonomy. It became a pivotal chapter, testing the resilience of our family's bonds. I was ostracised for being a wayward, defiant, and outspoken brat by some elders, while others remained neutral. However, you see, in the unfolding story, the choices made will echo through generations. As a mother, protector, and mediator, I found a path that preserves the essence of our family's harmony while respecting the individuality and wishes of my grieving daughter at that time. Today, Zivai's carefree spirit becomes a source of light, a counterpoint to the darker notes that once threatened to overshadow our family's harmony.

As a mother, I cherish her free-spirited nature, understanding that her love for tradition is not a constraint but a celebration of our shared heritage. Quite the opposite of her younger sister, Tarisai, who is a staunch Christian. Despite their differences, they both contribute uniquely to the grand mosaic of our family. In this mosaic, my carefree daughter is a vibrant thread—a reminder that amidst life's complexities, there's beauty in embracing the simplicity of tradition and the joy it brings.

In the symphony of our family's beliefs, I find myself sipping from a different cup—a choice that raises eyebrows within the framework of my daughter's staunch Christian convictions. My preference for beer becomes a subtle dissonance, a note out of tune with the harmony my daughter seeks in her faith. Yet, it is a personal choice, a sip of autonomy amidst the complex melodies of tradition and spirituality. As a bridge between worlds, I acknowledge the clash between our beliefs. My daughter's faith refrains from certain indulgences, while my own perspective on spirituality embraces the freedom to make individual choices. In the mix of our family's story, my occasional enjoyment of beer becomes a thread of tolerance, a reminder that diversity in beliefs can coexist without compromising the love and respect we share. It's a delicate dance, finding common ground amidst the contrasting notes of our beliefs. As the story unfolds, I hope our family can embrace the diversity of our individual melodies, creating a richer, more harmonious composition.

My father, Sansirai, a figure whose presence echoes in the background of our family's narrative—a soul whose absence shaped the cadence of my childhood. His footsteps, though silent now, once played a vital role in orchestrating the rhythms of our family life. A maestro in his own right, he instilled values that continue to resonate through generations. He was a soft-spoken man who became loud and rowdy after a few beers. A contrasting fit for Eti. His job at Lion Matches made him popular among smokers as he gifted them matchsticks every weekend. We never ran out of matchsticks to start a fire in our house. His departure left a void, a missing melody that weaves through our story. Yet, in the echoes of his teachings and the love he shared, he remains an enduring presence—an unseen conductor guiding us through life's symphony. As I walk the path of balancing tradition, spirituality, and the complexities of family, I draw upon the lessons he imparted—the importance of harmony, understanding, and unwavering love. In the grand composition of our family's story, my father is a poignant melody—a reminder that even in his physical absence, his essence endures, weaving through the fabric of our lives. He supported his wife throughout her journey as a spirit medium. As I reflect on his legacy, I find strength in the echoes of his wisdom, and I strive to pass on the harmonies he cultivated—a tribute to the enduring influence of a father whose spirit remains alive in the melody of our family's journey.

I remember that day when my mother took part in that ritual that almost cost her life, drinking the blood straight from the cow, I grappled with a spectrum of emotions. It was a scene deeply embedded in our cultural heritage, a practice passed down through generations.

There was a sense of respect for the history and significance behind the ritual—an acknowledgment of the spiritual connection forged by such traditions. Yet, simultaneously, there was an unsettling discomfort, a clash with contemporary sensibilities, including those upheld by the SPCA and other pro-animal beliefs, not to mention vegetarian and veterinarian perspectives.

The visceral nature of the ritual challenged my composure—a collision of the past and present, where the scent of blood mingled with the weight of cultural heritage. In the making of our family's story, these moments became poignant chords—a reminder that our journey was not only about embracing the harmonies but also navigating the dissonances that shaped our identity.

As events transpired, I found solace in the understanding that traditions, like melodies, carried different notes. It was in the delicate harmony of acceptance that I navigated the intricate dance between the past and the present. My mother, draped in ceremonial attire, stood beside the freshly slaughtered cow, a sacred ritual unfolding in the heart of the village. The air was heavy with the scent of watered gardens, mingling with the earthy aroma of the ritual site. Villagers, gathered in respectful silence, bore witness to an age-old tradition.

As people sang and other spirit mediums intoned ancient chants, my mother reached her mouth to the cow's throat. I watched as she consumed the warm blood of the sacrificed cow, its crimson hue mirroring the solemnity of the occasion. The murmurs of the crowd faded momentarily as the first sip was taken—a communion with the life force of the animal, a symbolic gesture connecting the living with the divine.

The moment was both sacred and raw, a visceral link to ancestral roots. I know Tarisai who was there, stood conflicted by the collision of tradition and modern sensibilities, and watched as her grandmother partook in this ancient rite, the act transcending the physical and delving into the spiritual realm.

The echoes of the chanting, the earthy scents, and the palpable weight of tradition hung in the air, creating a tableau of mixed emotions—a scene etched into the memory of many especially our family since my mother then fell sick suddenly. That day I questioned if it was worth continuing with her calling in the midst of so many enemies and such hatred. She nearly died in a flash. Seeing her staggering and struggling, refusing help even from her aide Miriam, broke me down. She had to undergo such rituals, yet in Tarisai's faith, she did not have to expose herself. Tarisai said back in the days, the Israelites made animal sacrifices, but after Jesus' sacrificial death on the cross, there was no need for that. He became their redemption. This was different. I know Tarisai had her fair share of enemies, but not to this magnitude. The ritual itself was not the issue, as it had been done safely since time immemorial. The fact that she was poisoned in such an intricate plot baffled me. She was attacked for her role as a spirit medium by her own brother; what more by strangers and neighbours. But she conquered. It is also said that the spirit of Pfumojena upon her saved her and fought for her. Good wins. That is what matters at the end of the day.

Chapter 26

I sometimes wonder how different things would have been if I had married Matamba. Despite that, I stand firm in my belief that had Emma succeeded in pursuing my father, I would have intervened forcefully, perhaps even physically. I even forgave Mangondi for what he did to us. I heard he now plays the news drum for the 8 pm main news in various styles, earning a substantial income from his talent. He boasts of being a descendant of Chaminuka and charges a salary double that of his peers.

These days, I find myself drinking from the green bottle not to get drunk, but simply to let my mind wander. I'm not one for confrontations; I prefer to rumble and ramble. Rambling has become my forte. I also find solace in scrolling through my phone. Tarisai gifted me a phone, and I've grown fond of taking selfies. Even my mother, Eti, now has a phone. We enjoy regularly calling each other, sharing laughter over Tarisai's experiences navigating marriage with Tikana. On a lighter note, there's the local gossip about Nancy, who was allegedly dating the headman under the guise of teaching his son English, despite suspicions lingering among the community. Well, I had my suspicions all along, but I've never been one to pry into others' lives. I have my own husband to dote over and little grandchildren to play with.

I told Tarisai as long as I could continue drinking beer now and then, I could be converted to Christianity. In all fairness, I saw nothing wrong with beer as long as one behaved, something which I upheld. Of course, there were few village imbeciles like Marufu who lost their tails after a sip. Uncle Mangondi had introduced me to the brown bottle and the green one. The brown one was called Black Label and the green ones were Zambezi and Bohlingers. Although I preferred my traditionally brewed beer, it was refreshing to have the lighter green bottles once in a while. Black label was flat and bitter in a dark way. I liked it.

I decided to join the Roman Catholic Church so they could sing at my requiem mass, Fr. Ribeiro's funeral song "Mutungamirireiwo Yesu" or the song "Mumureverere." Tarisai stuck with her Baptist Church. Tarisai was thrilled that I quit brewing beer. I still drank it and wine too.

"Does that give you joy that I quit brewing seven-days beer? Do you know how much sadness that news has brought to many? I have dealt my fellow countrymen a heavy blow," I sighed with a corky smile.

"Mum, it wouldn't paint a good picture at church. For years I struggled with that fact but we are obliged to love and obey our parents are we not? If I had my way, I would have thrown out all your beer making equipment, like how Jesus chased out and overturned the moneychangers' and vendors' tables in the temple." We both laughed as we often did whenever this chat came up. Tarisai had my sense of humour, but once angered, she was like a wounded lion.

Not all answers are solutions

Equilibrium